3 4143 10008 5545
D1135388

Crimespotting

Crimespotting

Lin Anderson, Kate Atkinson,
Margaret Atwood,
Christopher Brookmyre,
John Burnside, Isla Dewar,
A.L. Kennedy, Denise Mina,
Ian Rankin, James Robertson

Introduction by
Irvine Welsh

Foreword by
Rt Hon. George Grubb,
Lord Provost of Edinburgh

This edition published in Great Britain in 2009 by
Polygon, an imprint of Birlinn Ltd
West Newington House
10 Newington Road
Edinburgh
EH9 1QS

www.birlinn.co.uk

9 8 7 6 5 4 3 2 1

ISBN 978 1 84697 124 2

British Library Cataloguing-in-Publication Data
A catalogue record for this book is available on
request from the British Library.

Typeset by Palimpsest Book Production Limited,
Grangemeouth, Stirlingshire
Printed and bound in the UK by CPI Mackays, Chatham ME5 8TD

CONTENTS

FOREWORD

Welcome to *The OneCity Casebook*, the third anthology to be published in support of the OneCity Trust, and the biggest yet. When it was suggested that the next OneCity collection should be a book of crime stories, the editors decided to do something a little different and approach an eclectic range of authors from the Scottish crime writing community, and from far beyond, to see if they would like to write a new story set in Edinburgh and featuring a crime. The result is an astonishing line-up, showcasing some of the very best contemporary writers. The contributors each responded differently – some comically, some politically, some historically – but all unexpectedly. This is a book of crime stories in the broadest possible sense – not a book of clichés.

It is often said that crime fiction holds a mirror up to society; and what we see when we look at Edinburgh is a city full of beauty and potential, but riven with inequality. The OneCity Trust is committed to tackling the poverty that causes exclusion – the poverty of resources, of expectation, of opportunity, of care and understanding – by funding grass-roots projects which empower individual communities to work for social justice. One of the great benefits of literature is that it can open our eyes to lives beyond the narrow compass of our own and expand our sympathies for those on the margins. This book has another aim as well: to raise funds which can make a tangible difference here in Edinburgh.

My first thanks go to Ian Rankin, an Ambassador of the OneCity Trust, who has done so much to establish Edinburgh at the forefront of contemporary fiction. This collection has been brought together under his inspiration, and would not have been possible without him. Secondly, to Irvine Welsh, also one of the Trust's Ambassadors, and an iconic chronicler of our city, for his heartfelt introduction.

To each of the authors, we owe an immense debt of gratitude: they have not only given generously of their time and their extraordinary talents, but have also agreed to donate all royalties to the OneCity Trust.

Finally, to you, the reader. By buying this book, you are ensuring that the vital work of the Trust can continue. Thank you.

Rt Hon. George Grubb
LORD PROVOST OF EDINBURGH

Find out more about the work of the Trust at
www.onecity.org.uk

INTRODUCTION

In the part of Edinburgh where I grew up, a small group of people viewed criminal activity as a legitimate business. They were always very much a minority in the community: generally tolerated, occasionally indulged, but more usually frowned upon. There were a few of what the authorities, back in those casually pejorative days, used to term 'problem families', but even the most hardworking, salt-of-the-earth ones, like I perceived my own to be, were blessed with the odd interesting black sheep, who tended to play quite hard and fast with the property laws. As a boy, I was drawn to these characters; they told the best stories, and I was always a sucker for a good story.

I might be guilty of romanticising the memory of community that existed in Edinburgh's peripheral housing schemes back in the 1970s, as people are prone to do with regard to their childhoods. But there is little doubt that this sense of society collapsed in the 1980s, to such an extent that it's now practically unrecognisable. Mass unemployment and underemployment, growing social and economic inequities through the sale of high amenity council stock, abysmal educational opportunities and the influx of drugs, have all conspired to change completely the nature of the poorer parts of British cities in the last generation, and Edinburgh is no exception. In its place is the black economy, which is now, sadly, the only real option for so many of our young people. Basically, in a consumer society there is more to steal. While many are desperately poor, this great wealth is flaunted before us all. Even when crime does not have an obvious economic gain, it's often generated by boredom, itself the product of poor finances, undereducation and underemployment. Resisting the temptation to become a participant in some kind of illegal activity requires an almost iron will for marginalised youth in the poorest areas of our cities. This lure is everywhere, usually winning by default, as the opportunity for anything else is practically non-existent.

We're all experts on crime – or at least if you trawl the bars, golf clubs and coffee shops of Britain, that's the impression you'd most likely be left with. And certainly, we're bombarded with enough of it in the media. But most people who read crime fiction tend to be honest citizens, who will never commit a felony. They are also far less likely to be victims of crime. Conversely, ask any prison librarian, and they will tell you that convicts do not read crime novels, but accounts of 'True Crime'. In some ways it's comforting that criminals are like everybody else; they just want to be better at what they do. The best places, ironically, to enhance your criminal skills are those universities of crime we call prisons.

What about the writers? Well, speaking personally, I've found that crime writers tend to be among the most cheerful and good-natured of all the members of this diverse group of strange souls who elect to make our living telling stories. This can be evidenced by the fact that so many of them have stepped forward to make contibutions to this anthology, possibly against the wishes of their agents, who might rather hope they worked on their next book, to build the franchise in what is a highly competitive and lucrative market.

But the great thing about this collection is that it not only includes some of the undisputed masters of the genre, all of them on top form, but surprise choices not known for writing what marketing by publishers and booksellers has conditioned us to refer to as 'crime fiction'. It certainly embraces many writers who are among my personal favourites.

What then, about us, the crime readers? Well, I like to think that we're looking for more than just a vicarious thrill. I think we crave what real life so seldom delivers, the promise of resolution in a world full of uncertainty.

On that note, I was very proud when I was asked to be an ambassador for the One CityTrust, which seeks to foster social inclusion and opportunity in our all-too-divided city. In 2005, Alexander McCall Smith, Ian Rankin, J. K. Rowling and myself produced a book, which proved a popular way to launch the project. Some writers of children's fiction then came together to compose another one, *Our City*. Now we have a third, which, given the star-studded lineup and quality of the story-telling, I'm sure will be widely enjoyed. At the risk of sounding a bit of a preachy bore, I think it's important that we realise, even as we are being entertained by the virtuoso skills of these great writers, that with regard to the nature of the OneCity Trust, for many people, crime is not a form of entertainment. Sadly, it's a way of life.

It doesn't have to be this way, and the OneCity Trust is supporting projects that are helping to ensure that for at least some people, it won't be the case. So I'd like to end by extending a genuine and heartfelt thanks to everybody who bought a copy of this book, and to all the exceptional pensmiths who gave up their time to produce it.

Irvine Welsh

Affairs of The Heart

KATE ATKINSON

Franklin met Connie one evening outside the Queen's Hall. It was raining and when Connie slipped on the wet pavement Franklin helped her up and offered the shelter of his umbrella. 'It was incredibly romantic,' she said afterwards. 'Like something out of Forster.' Franklin happened to have been walking past when Connie was coming out of the Beethoven recital, but in her uncharacteristically flustered state she received the impression that he had also been at the concert.

'It was wonderful, wasn't it?' she said to him fifteen minutes later in the Café Royal. 'How challenging Beethoven's late string quartets are,' she added, decorously sipping a glass of Merlot.

'Yet how rewarding,' Franklin said. He had never been to a classical concert in his life and certainly hadn't listened to a Beethoven string quartet, late or otherwise.

Connie seemed eager to share the details of her life with him. She was twenty-eight years old, educated at St George's and then at Aberdeen University and now worked as an account handler in an advertising agency in Leith. She was the second in a clutch of three girls, Patience, Constance and Faith. ('Mummy', apparently, was a stalwart churchwoman who believed in virtue.) 'No Charity?' Franklin said and Connie said, 'No, and don't mention Hope to Mummy if you meet her.'

'My sister, Patience, is a cellist with the RSNO,' Connie continued blithely. 'And Faith is a senior registrar at the

Royal Infirmary. Daddy's a heart surgeon and Mummy does–' at this point Connie made rabbit ears, something Franklin particularly disliked '–"good works". She's a very keen gardener too. Her roses are legendary.'

Franklin in a nutshell. *Ab ovo*. English. Thirty-four years old, five foot ten, one hundred and fifty pounds. Eyes of blue, hair of brown. Born in a Swiss clinic beneath the benign and sunny sign of the Lion three weeks after his father was immolated in the Austrian Grand Prix. His much-married mother, the slovenly scion of a minor, ruined aristocratic family, was notorious for having been involved in a sleazy sex-scandal *(Top Totty Brings Down Government*, according to one tabloid headline at the time).

Franklin left London for Scotland, managing to scrape into Stirling University on a media studies course, and after graduation he joined a local radio station from which starting point he climbed, like a salmon up a ladder, to the dizzy heights of being a script editor on a Scottish TV soap, *Green Acres* – a violent yet couthy mix, as if *The Sopranos* had relocated to *Brigadoon* and all the script editors had media studies degrees from Stirling.

Franklin felt that one day he would be tested, that a challenge would appear out of the blue – a war, a quest, a disaster – and that he would rise to this challenge and not be found wanting. It would be the making of him, he would come into his own. But what if this never happened, what if nothing was asked of him? Would he have to ask it of himself? And how did you do that?

Franklin was also unbelievably unlucky, descended from a long line of bad luck, only child of an only child of an only child and so on, and had become reconciled to the fact that no matter how many times the wheel of fortune turned he would always find himself stuck on the underside like gum on a shoe. Connie seemed like the very person who might change his luck.

'What does *your* family do, Franklin?' Connie asked.

Franklin, unfortunately, had only his lone, infamous parent to offer.

'There's just my mother, I'm afraid,' he said. 'She's' (he made rabbit ears) '"a widow".'

Franklin was surprised when less than an hour after leaving the pub he found himself naked on the beech laminate flooring of Connie's basement flat in Cumberland Street, kissing her grazed knees in an odd combination of first aid and foreplay. Their modest intake of wine, the Beethoven and her generally demure demeanour had led him to think that Connie wasn't the kind of girl who kissed on a first date, let alone shed her clothes before she'd hardly got the key in her front door. He said something to this effect to her afterwards when they were lying in a tangled, sweaty knot on her 'Beware of the Cat' doormat and she laughed and said, 'Of *course* I'm not that kind of girl, but it's not every day you fall – literally – head over heels in love.' Franklin felt both alarmed and flattered in equal measure by this statement.

It turned out that Connie had the easygoing nature of a girl who had never had a worry in her life greater than whether or not flat shoes made her calves look fat. She was 'almost a vegetarian', did Pilates twice a week and played for the Edinburgh Netball Club. She was thrillingly well-organised with no self-doubt whatsoever. For Franklin, a person continually in the throes of an apprehensive nihilism, this last was a compelling quality. Furthermore, Connie's hair was straight and brown and never seemed to tangle, her breath was always slightly minty no matter the time of day and she was possessed of the kind of flawless complexion that you only got from a clear conscience.

Conversations with Connie tended to be based on an endless series of ethical dilemmas. Franklin knew it was a test he was bound to fail eventually. 'If I was trapped in a burning building with a cat, which of us would you rescue?' Connie asked as they came out of the Cameo cinema.

'You, of course,' Franklin said without hesitation.

'What about the cat?'

'What *about* the cat?'

'You would just leave it to burn to death, Franklin?

They pursued a hectic month of courtship. It was an exhausting and somehow very public chase – theatres, cinemas, museums, cafés, endless meals out in restaurants. On top of that there were race meetings in Musselburgh, walks in the Botanics and Holyrood Park, athletic ascents of Arthur's Seat. Connie seemed particularly fond of the outdoors. Franklin would have preferred to have stayed home and had sex, although, thankfully, Connie's diary managed to make room for a lot of that too.

Franklin found it difficult to keep up with Connie –

literally – when they were out together, rather than being intimately coupled up, arm in arm, Connie was always shooting ahead (he'd never met anyone who walked so fast), leaving him trailing behind. He hoped the pace would slow down soon.

Barely a month after meeting Connie, Franklin found himself meeting 'Mummy and Daddy' for the first time, invited for the weekend to their house in Cramond.

'Sherry?' Mr Kingshott asked, hefting a heavy crystal decanter. ('Daddy can be a wee bit gruff,' Connie had murmured, to Franklin's alarm, as they made their way up the Kingshotts' impressive drive.)

'Thank you,' Franklin said. He felt acutely conscious of his manners in this delicate environment. It seemed inevitable that something would be broken. Drinking sherry before lunch – lunch itself – was just one of the many attractive things that Connie would bring to his life if he married her. He would swim in the Kingshott gene pool like a happy sun-kissed otter.

Mr Kingshott was smaller than Franklin had expected, a little gamecock of a man, strutting around his lovely Cramond drawing-room, pecking at his brood. Franklin felt that if he were going to have his heart operated on he would prefer it to be done by a bigger man, a man whose hand was large enough to hold his heart firmly without any danger of it slipping from his overly-petite fingers. He also felt that he would not like his heart to be tended by a man who continually grunted and sighed with irritation and impatience, Mrs Kingshott apparently being the usual beneficiary of this malcontent. ('Daddy's a bit of a tyrant,' Connie said cheerfully.) Franklin thought that he would like the man operating on his heart to be singing, light opera, nothing too dramatic, Gilbert and Sullivan perhaps.

'Mummy!' Connie exclaimed as a rather large, soft woman entered the drawing-room, holding a wooden spoon in her hand as if it were a wand. She had the distracted air of someone who had wandered into a room without having the slightest idea why she was there.

Mummy smiled sadly at Franklin as if she knew some terrible thing that was to befall him and then wandered out of the room again, spoon aloft.

All of Mummy's brood had pitched up at the Cramond house ('The nest full again,' Connie said.) 'So we can meet the beau,' Patience said. Patience was both the eldest and the largest of the three sisters. (No Chekhovian gloom in the Kingshott household, no longing for a golden somewhere else, Franklin was relieved to note. Except possibly from Mummy.) Patience, in Birkenstocks and a paisley blouse, had a suggestion of heaviness about her, as if one day she would be in possession of the stout figure and bovine slowness of her mother. Faith, the youngest, on the other hand, had her father's height and his bird-boned frame. Franklin was struck by the sight of the three sisters together, Patience was too big and serious, Faith too small and flighty, but Connie was, in the wise words of Goldilocks, just right. If he could love anyone, surely it would be her.

'Have a seat,' Connie said, indicating a sofa that wouldn't have looked out of place in a royal palace. It was more a mansion than a house. There was a library and a tennis court, endless well-kept lawns.

'Mind the cat,' Connie said hastily as Franklin narrowly missed sitting on what he had taken to be some kind of strange cushion but which turned out to be a dish-faced, long-haired white cat that glared malevolently at him. 'Pedigree,' Patience muttered, as if that explained everything.

Patience, who clearly lacked Connie's sunny nature, downed a schooner of sherry in one and said to Franklin, 'If you were a musical instrument what musical instrument would you be, Franklin?' She seemed to regard the question as one of real interest. She had a kind of Germanic earnestness about her that made Franklin feel shallow.

All three sisters stared at him, waiting for an answer. 'Violin,' he hazarded. To say 'Cello' would have seemed sycophantic, given that it was Patience's own instrument. A violin seemed a safe bet, like the cello it had strings, and it wasn't quirky like a bassoon or a tuba or grandstanding like a piano, but Patience raised her eyebrows at his answer as if he'd just fulfilled her expectations by saying something banal.

Franklin was relieved when they moved into the dining-room and settled at the (enormous) table. Mrs Kingshott carried in a platter and ceremoniously presented a poached salmon (one dull eye glared out at them) to Mr Kingshott. The salmon, apparently, fitted happily into Connie's 'almost vegetarian' philosophy. Mr Kingshott dissected the fish as if he were conducting a post-mortem. Franklin found himself wondering what Connie would taste like if he bit through her smooth skin and into the firm yet tender flesh beneath. The breast of an Aylesbury duck or a particularly good pork sausage perhaps. Franklin realised that the very fact that he had thoughts like this made him incredibly unsuitable to be in possession of the Kingshotts' middle child. He suspected that in her parents' eyes (and in his own too if he was honest) he must seem feckless and totally unworthy of the gift of their daughter.

'What is it you actually *do*, Franklin?' Mr Kingshott asked suddenly, as if he'd been struggling with this quandary since the sherry. For a moment Franklin thought this might also be some kind of game (*If you were a job what job would you be?*) 'For a living,' Mr Kingshott clarified when Franklin looked blank.

'Oh,' Franklin said. 'I work in television.'

'Television?' Mr Kingshott repeated, his face contorted as if he was in some kind of exquisite pain. Previously Franklin had always felt a certain amount of pride when announcing this fact, it had taken him a long time to squirm his way up to where he was now. 'On *Green Acres*,' he added.

'A farming programme?' Mr Kingshott looked incredulous, as well he might. 'You?'

'Oh, Daddy,' Mummy laughed. 'It's a soap opera, everyone knows that. Daddy likes Wagner,' she said to Franklin, as if that explained everything.

'Mummy's an addict, Frankie,' Faith said.

'God,' Franklin said to Mrs Kingshott, 'how awful for you.'

'Of *Green Acres*,' Connie said.

'Of course,' Franklin said.

He suddenly realised that Faith was studying his face

across the centrepiece of yellow roses ('St Alban,' Mummy said) as if he were a fascinating new life form. He felt something rubbing against his calf and wondered if it was the cat again. He glanced down and was shocked to see a naked foot, the scarlet nails like drops of blood, arching and contracting as it stroked the denim of his jeans. The foot could only belong to Faith unless Patience, sitting at the other end of the table, possessed freakishly long legs. Perhaps he wouldn't be such a happy otter if Connie's sisters were in the pool with him, circling like sharks.

'So, Frankie,' Faith purred, 'If you were a disease what disease would you be?'

★

There was a mutually declared break before the appearance of a raspberry mille-feuille that was waiting rather anxiously in the wings. 'I really wasn't in the mood for pastry-making,' Mummy said, frowning at the yellow roses as if they were about to do something unpredictable.

'Still on the Prozac, Mummy?' Patience said. ('Daddy fills all Mummy's prescriptions,' Connie said.)

Connie leaned closer to Franklin. She smelt fresh and flowery. 'Let's go outside,' she said.

'Mummy's pride and joy,' Connie said, rather brutally snapping off a delicate rose the colour of peaches and cream and holding it beneath Franklin's nose. It was a lovely perfume, the inside of old wardrobes, China tea on a summer lawn, Connie's skin. 'Pretty Lady,' she said.

'You are,' Franklin affirmed.

'No, it's the name of the rose,' Connie said. 'I think we should get married.'

For some reason, Franklin's dumbfounded silence was taken as an affirmative and the next thing he knew he was lost in a shrieking scrum of Kingshott women, only Mr Kingshott, more interested in the raspberry mille-feuille, remained aloof from the hysteria. Franklin wasn't sure why they were shrieking. He wondered if it was horror. 'Just like Jane Austen,' Connie said, fanning her flushed face with her hand.

Seeing that a romantic gesture was expected of him, Franklin drove back into town, put a thousand pounds on a handy little bay running in the last race at Beverley that came in at 10/1, strolled down the street with a winner's easy gait and bought a diamond engagement ring from Alistair Tait, the jeweller. ('Any vices, Franklin?' Mr Kingshott had asked with mock amiability after the celebratory champagne was opened and the raspberry mille-feuille was finally consumed. 'Oh, just the usual,' Franklin laughed.)

On his return, Mr Kingshott coerced Franklin into a game of tennis on the hard court at the back of the house. 'Reach for it, boy!' Mr Kingshott yelled at him, lobbing an impossible ball high over Franklin's head towards the back of the court. Despite his size, Mr Kingshott, it turned out later, was the doyen of the local tennis club, whereas Franklin hadn't played since listlessly knocking a ball about at university.

Mr Kingshott took great pleasure in reporting back,

over an elaborate afternoon tea that Mummy had prepared, that he had 'soundly trounced' Franklin. 'Well, Daddy wouldn't play anything he couldn't win,' Connie said later to Franklin as if that was the most reasonable thing in the world.

By the time they had eaten a supper of chicken sandwiches and drunk more champagne (they seemed to do nothing but eat and drink) Franklin couldn't wait to retreat to the attic guest-room. Kingshott daughters were not allowed to share a bed with their beaux beneath the family roof. ('Daddy likes to pretend that we're all virgins.')

Franklin opened the door to the little room under the eaves and nearly had a heart attack. A figure was standing quite still at the open casement window, gazing out at the darkness. The figure turned round and to Franklin's relief it was only Mrs Kingshott.

'Mrs Kingshott?' Franklin said softly. For an awful moment he wondered if she was thinking of jumping.

'Oh, Franklin,' she said as if she was surprised to see him. 'I was just . . .' she gestured vaguely at the narrow single-bed. She was holding a carafe of water and a glass which she placed gently down on the bedside table. She moved carefully like someone made of something breakable. She sat on the bed and stroked the cover as if it were a sick animal. 'Sometimes I wish . . .' she said.

'What do you wish for, Mrs Kingshott?'

'Oh, nothing. Silly me,' she said. 'It's just . . .' she sighed, a tremulous, sob-bearing sigh, and absentmindedly plumped up the pillows on the bed. 'You know. The death of hope.'

Franklin tried to think of something to say that would

mollify this rather bleak existential statement but Mummy jumped up and said brightly, 'Night, night, Franklin.'

Soundly asleep, Franklin incorporated the opening of the squeaking bedroom door into a dream he was in the midst of. The monstrous but indeterminate predator that had been hunting him through an abandoned railway goods yard was closing in on him. He could hear its ragged breath, could feel the heat of it, the strange, soft texture of it. It was smaller than he had imagined but it wrapped itself around him and started to probe and pull at his body with its small hands. Perhaps not a monster but an alien? Without warning, it thrust its tongue into his mouth. He screamed the mute scream of the nightmare victim.

'It's alright, Frankie,' a familiar female voice said quietly in his ear. 'It's just the doctor here to examine you.'

There was a festive air about the house the next morning. 'Not every day we manage to get one of them off our hands,' Mr Kingshott said, over an extensive cooked breakfast. 'Although, of course, no man should marry, Balzac says, until he has studied anatomy and dissected at least one woman.'

Franklin tried very hard not to catch faithless Faith's eye over the table. He needn't have worried, she hardly gave him a second glance and if it hadn't been for the scratches and the teeth-marks on his body (more wildcat than woman) he might have dismissed last night as the nightmare that it was.

'Sleep well?' Connie said, kissing him lightly on the

cheek before sitting down at the table. Franklin almost choked on his guilt.

Mummy slid a fried egg onto his plate and patted him on the shoulder as if he was a dog.

Franklin felt compelled to accompany Connie and Mrs Kingshott to church.

'Then you can meet the minister who'll be marrying us.'

She spent most of the service admiring her ring in the sunlight that cascaded through the church windows while Franklin weighed his soul and found it sadly wanting.

More sherry before lunch. Franklin hadn't realised what a potent drink it was.

'Fetch another bottle from the kitchen, would you?' Mr Kingshott said to Franklin in the same tone of voice he might have used with a waiter.

The big six-door Aga that Mrs Kingshott treated with a mixture of servitude and fear (much the same relationship as she had with Mr Kingshott) was pumping out heat on what was an already stifling day. Mrs Kingshott was putting the finishing touches to a peach pavlova.

'Can I do something to help?' Franklin asked. He felt strangely compelled to treat Mrs Kingshott like an invalid.

She shook her head in a tragic way as if to say no but then said, 'That's very kind of you. Perhaps you could slice a lemon for me?'

'Of course,' Franklin said. He felt strangely comfortable with Mrs Kingshott (or 'Mummy' as he had begun to think of her). How much better off he would have been with a mother like Mrs Kingshott. She would have sent him to scout camps and concert performances of *A Young Person's Guide to the Orchestra* and given him sound advice, unlike his own mother ('Remember the rule of the three Fs, Franklin – if it flies, floats or fucks, then, for God's sake, *rent it*').

Mrs Kingshott handed him a knife to cut the lemon with, holding it delicately at the edges of the handle as if she was worried that she might suddenly turn it on herself.

They lunched al fresco on a roast chicken, a bird which was also nearly vegetarian, apparently. Mr Kingshott wielded the carving knife as if it were a particularly large scalpel.

'Breast or leg?' he asked Franklin. 'Which do you prefer?' For a confusing moment Franklin though that he was somehow referring to his daughters.

'Leg,' Franklin said, incapable of saying the word 'breast' to Mr Kingshott when surrounded by his flock of women. Mr Kingshott passed Franklin the delicately carved slices of dark meat and said, 'No breast? Sure?'

'Sure,' Franklin said.

The peach pavlova made its entrance before the chicken had exited. Faith ripped the wishbone from the remains of the bird (it was hard to believe that someone so savage had received the same upbringing as Connie) and held out the little bony arch and said, 'Make a wish, Frankie,' but before he could even begin to think of anything he wanted to wish for (where to start?) Faith had yanked aggressively on the fragile bone and claimed the greater part. Franklin could see a little shred of chicken flesh lodged between her front teeth. He hoped she was never in a position to perform a medical procedure on him.

'Then Aunt Jefferson and Mr Bray,' Mummy said. 'And all of the string section,' Patience said. It took Franklin a while to realise it was his own wedding that was being discussed.

'Who's on your guest list, Franklin?' Connie asked. 'There's your mother, of course,' she reminded him before he could answer. The thought of his mother at the wedding filled Franklin with feverish horror. The only thing that was certain was that it all would go badly. If only Franklin had told Connie that he was an orphan. Perhaps he could put his mother in a coma, it was always a handy device in *Green Acres*, when you wanted to shelve a cast member for a while. And his mother was pretty much a soap opera character anyway.

'Patience and Faith will be the bridesmaids, of course,' Connie was saying to her mother. 'It's just a shame they're different heights.'

'You could cut Patience's feet off,' Faith suggested.

'Or stretch Faith,' Patience said.

Mrs Kingshott stood up from the table suddenly and said, 'There should be three bridesmaids.' Connie reached out for her hand and tried to get her to sit down again.

'Come on, Mummy,' Faith said, surprisingly gentle. 'Don't get upset.'

'Sit down,' Mr Kingshott barked at his wife. 'And don't start all that nonsense again.'

Mrs Kingshott stood rigid and wild-eyed, like some terrible figure in a Greek tragedy. A dramatic clap of thunder exploded overhead and the heavens opened. From the look of her, Mrs Kingshott would still have been out there at bedtime and it took the persuasive powers of all three girls to coax her indoors. The pavlova was left to melt in the rain, the peach slices like beached fish in the surf.

'What was all that about?' Franklin asked later.

'Hope,' Connie said.

'Hope?'

'Our sister, the youngest. She died of meningitis when she was five. Mummy wanted to take her to hospital but Daddy said she was making a fuss about nothing and it was just a fever. Hope died in Mummy's arms.'

'That's *terrible*,' Franklin said, fresh to the tragedy.

'Yes,' Connie said. 'It is, isn't it? Daddy's such a brute. You have no idea,' she added, staring at something out of sight.

'So let me get this right, the building's on fire and I have to choose between rescuing a cat and rescuing the cure for cancer?'

'Yes,' Connie said.

'And I definitely can't save both?'

'No.'

'Is it the cure for all cancers? Or just some?'

'All.'

'Is the cat old?'

'What difference does that make? Is its life worth less because it's old? Will it suffer less when it's burnt alive?'

Franklin wondered if Connie's hypothetical cat was a distant relative of Schrödinger's Cat. 'And you're definitely not in the building? It's just a straight choice – cat or cancer? Cancer or cat?'

'Yes.'

'Where are *you*? Just out of interest?'

'I'm standing on the pavement watching, Franklin.'

Mr Kingshott retired to the gloom of the library while the women of the household embarked on a furiously paced game of Monopoly in the course of which even Mrs Kingshott became a cut-throat (*Park Lane! Mine!*)

Franklin excused himself and dozed on the sofa. He did feel extraordinarily tired and woozy and the Kingshotts' sofa was as comfy as a fairy-tale feather bed.

When he woke, the drawing-room was empty, no sign of any Kingshotts and the Monopoly board had been tidied away. It felt late and Franklin wondered how long he had slept. The clock on the mantelpiece said eight o'clock but surely someone would have woken him to partake in the endless round of eating and drinking that seemed to go on in the house.

There was no sign of life anywhere and Franklin wandered from room to room, occasionally shouting 'Hello?' to the air until only the library remained unexplored. Franklin paused before the closed door. The idea of disturbing the bear in his lair was unnerving. He put his ear to the door. There was no sound from within. Perhaps Mr Kingshott had jumped ship with his women. Franklin knocked sharply twice and when there was no answer he turned the handle and opened the door cautiously, half-expecting to find Bluebeard's wives hanging from butchers' hooks.

There was nothing, a faint tang in the air, iron and salt and something faintly raw.

And a foot. A smallish foot, poking out from behind the desk. A foot encased in a beige wool sock and a tan handmade brogue that looked very like one that Mr Kingshott was wearing the last time Franklin saw him.

Franklin approached the desk and discovered that the foot was (thankfully) still attached to the rest of Mr Kingshott. Unfortunately, there was a knife sticking out of his chest, exactly where his heart was. It seemed an ironic death for a man who spent his life sticking knives into other people's hearts.

Mr Kingshott's eyes were open, as fixed and dull as a dead salmon. It was just like Cluedo, Franklin thought – Mr Kingshott in the library with a dagger. Not a dagger exactly but a small sharp knife, very like the one Franklin had used earlier to slice a lemon for Mrs Kingshott, although, when he thought about it now, the lemon had never made an appearance at lunch.

Franklin's feet were sticking to the carpet and he realised he had walked in Mr Kingshott's blood. He felt sick. He knew he should phone the police but his brain was still fogged up. Had he been drugged? Faith must be pretty handy with narcotics.

He retreated to the hallway and was fumbling in his pocket for his mobile when the front door burst open and several policemen rushed in, followed by all the Kingshott women.

'That's him,' Patience said, pointing dramatically at Franklin.

'Yes,' Connie said, 'that's definitely him. He's been

stalking me for weeks, everywhere I go he follows.' She was a stagy actress, Franklin noted.

'We have photographs,' Patience said in her own histrionic style. It was like being in the middle of a poor amateur dramatic production. *An Inspector Calls*. From nowhere Patience produced a folder of black-and-white photographs. Franklin managed to catch a glimpse of them over the shoulder of one of the policemen. They all seemed to show Franklin loitering in Connie's wake in a variety of venues he recognised – Holyrood Park, George Street, coming out of the Lyceum. 'I was trying to catch up with her, not follow her,' he protested.

'Daddy tried to warn him off,' Connie said

'And so he killed him,' Faith said. 'Obviously.'

The cat appeared suddenly, arching its back and spitting at Franklin.

'He's an awfully good judge of character,' Connie said.

'Mrs Kingshott?' one of the policemen said, turning to her, as if she had some kind of casting vote on Franklin's fate.

Mrs Kingshott gazed into Franklin's face and gave a tremendous sigh. 'I'm afraid so,' she said. 'He's been giving us all so much bother.'

Franklin had an unnerving flashback to last night and the condom that Faith had produced and magicked away when she had finished ravishing him. He remembered the rabid biting and scratching – how many samples of DNA had she managed to steal off him? He had stood in Mr Kingshott's blood, his own bloody footprints tracking his journey all the way from the body. And what about the knife. He remembered the delicate way Mrs

Kingshott had handed it to him, so that no prints were on that knife except his.

'I thought you loved me,' Franklin said to Connie. Even to his own ears he sounded pathetic.

'He's so deluded,' Patience said to the policemen.

'I believe the medical term is erotomania,' Faith said. 'It often leads to violence, I'm afraid.'

'Don't listen to them!' Franklin said.

All four women stood on the doorstep and watched as Franklin was bundled into a police car. By now the place was swarming with more police, with forensics, with photographers, although it was a relatively subdued crime scene compared with anything in *Green Acres*. Franklin made a mental note for future use. If he had a future.

As the car drove away, Franklin caught sight of Mrs Kingshott. She gave him a regretful smile and waved goodbye to him.

Franklin waved back. Even now, he found himself not wanting to hurt Mummy's feelings.

Pretend Blood

MARGARET ATWOOD

Marla got into Past Lives through Sal. They were friends at work – they often had lunch together, and went shopping, and sometimes to movies, with nothing unusual being said. But one day Sal confided to Marla that in a past life she'd been Cleopatra. The reason she was telling Marla this was that she'd just got engaged – out came a hulking diamond – because she'd run into a man through an internet chat site who'd been Marc Antony, and they'd got together in real life, and needless to say they'd fallen in love, and wasn't that wonderful?

Marla nearly choked on her coffee. First of all, if Sal had been Cleopatra she herself had been the Queen of Sheba, because Sal wasn't exactly anyone's idea of Miss Sexy Ancient Egypt – she was thirty-five and tubby, with a pasty complexion and an overbite. Also, Marla had seen that play – a long time ago, granted, but not so long that she didn't remember the death of Marc Antony, and also that of Cleopatra, what with the asps in a basket.

'It didn't end very well, the first time,' she managed to croak out. It was cruel to laugh at someone else's nutty illusion, so she managed not to do that. Anyway, who was she to laugh? Nutty illusion or not, the Cleopatra thing had got results for Sal.

'That's true,' Sal said. 'It was awful at the time.' She gave a little shudder. Then she explained that the good thing about having a past life was that you got the chance to return to earth as the same person you'd once been, but this time you could make things come out better. Which was why so many of the Past Lifers were historic figures who'd had tragic finales. A lot were from the Roman Empire, for instance. And kings and queens, and dukes and duchesses – they'd been prone to trouble because of their ambition and other people's jealousy of them and so forth.

'How did you know?' asked Marla. 'That you were Cleopatra?'

'It just kind of came over me,' said Sal. 'The first time I saw a pyramid – well, not a pyramid, a photo of a pyramid – it looked so kind of familiar. And I've always had this fear of snakes.'

So has half the population, thought Marla. Better you should have a fear of Marc Antony: you're marrying an obvious wacko. Most likely a serial killer with a bunch of former Cleopatras stacked up in the cellar like cordwood. But her scepticism faded when she actually met Marc, whose name in this life was Bob, and he turned out to be perfectly nice, though a lot older and richer than Sal; and darned if Sal and Bob, or Marc, didn't get married after all, and take off for a new life in Scotland, where Bob lived. The climate there wasn't very Egyptian, but that didn't bother Sal: there were many sad parts about her past life she'd just as soon forget, she told Marla, and spending too much time in Egypt might be depressing for them both. Though they did intend to take a vacation there for a bit of nostalgia. Sal wanted to revisit her ancient barge trips, because those had been pretty splendid.

Before leaving for her new married life, Sal told Marla the name of the internet chat site – PLAYS, for Past Lives

And Your Self – and said Marla should give it a try: she had a feeling in her bones that Marla too was an Old Soul. Anyway, said Sal, Marla had nothing to lose, meaning she wasn't getting any younger, and unlike Sal – the new Sal – she had a dead-end job and no man in sight. Marla hadn't missed that gloating subtext. It irritated her.

*

It took Marla a while to seek out PLAYS, and she felt like an idiot even considering it – with my luck I'll meet Jack the Ripper, she thought – but she finally went online. It cost fifty dollars to join, and then you had to read the rules and pledge to abide by them. No duels with former enemies, for instance, and no questioning anyone else's identity, not even if there were two or three of someone. There were several Anne Boleyns, for instance, but the claimants got around that by being Anne at different times of her life – while courted by Henry, while pregnant, while waiting in the Tower to get her head chopped off. The feelings you'd have during such phases would be very different, so each set of feelings might have come back into a different present-day person. That was the PLAYS rationale.

Once you'd swallowed the initial premise, or pretended to – which was what Marla herself did – Past Lives turned out to be surprisingly entertaining. Sort of like a virtual masquerade ball: by being someone else, you could be more truly yourself. At first Marla held back, and merely listened in while other people exchanged historical factoids and favourite recipes – syllabub, sack posset, stuffed peacock. She watched friendships form, she watched flirtations – Henry the Fourth with Eleanor of Aquitaine, Marianne Evans with George Henry Lewes. Couples went off into private cubicles where they could have one-on-ones. She longed to know what happened to such pairings. Sometimes there would be an announcement – an engagement, or a wedding, like Sal's – but not very often.

To participate more actively, as she now longed to do, she needed more than a password: she needed a past life of her own. But how to decide which one? Marla suspected by now that PLAYS might be merely a kinky dating agency; even so, it could be crucially important who she chose to be, or to have been. She didn't want to end up playing Eva Braun to some psychopath's Adolf Hitler, though this duo had in fact flitted briefly across the screen.

She surprised herself by plunging into Mary Stewart, Queen of Scots. She'd had no prior interest, she didn't have any preparation for it – she chose it because both their names began with M and she'd once had a crush on a man named Stewart – but once she was in, she found herself getting caught up in the part. After she declared herself, she started receiving messages from several Elizabeth the Firsts. 'Were you really plotting against me?' said one. 'We could have been such good friends, we had so much in common.' 'I so much regret what happened,' said another. 'I felt terrible about the whole beheading thing. It was all a mistake.' 'The lead coffin was not my idea,' said a third. 'Well, anyway, your son inherited. And your embroidered elephant still exists. So it's not all bad.'

What lead coffin? thought Marla. What embroidered elephant? She went off to read up. You did learn a lot on PLAYS – it was an education in itself.

★

Marla kept up with Sal via email. At first the bulletins were short and bubbly. She and Bob/Marc had a lovely house, the garden flourished so well in that climate, Bob was so attentive, and so lavish. In return, Marla proffered her newfound Queen Maryness, though she was a little miffed when Sal didn't respond with the enthusiasm she'd expected.

Meanwhile, she got several rude messages from a John Knox, and met a David Rizzio – in the flesh, they went to a concert – who turned out to be gay but fun, and she turned down dating invitations from several Darnleys: the man had been a snot in his past life and surely wouldn't be any better now. But she accepted an Earl of Bothwell who'd looked like sort of a hunk, and had three martinis with him in a lava bar, and had almost got raped.

She felt she was beginning to understand the character of Mary from the inside. She was also leading a more interesting and varied life than she'd led in years. Still, despite that, nothing much to show.

★

After a silence of several months, she got a doleful email from Sal. Bob/Marc had fallen off a boat, on the Nile. He'd drowned. His arthritis, or else a crocodile, may have been involved. Sal was heartbroken: they never should have gone back there, it was bad luck for them. Would Marla like to come over on her vacation, to Edinburgh, just to be with Sal at this difficult time in her life? She, Sal, would pay for the ticket, she had lots of money now. Anyway, Sal thought Marla might like to see the ancient city where she herself had undergone such extremely crucial experiences, once upon a time.

Marla quickly accepted. Her vacation was two months away, so she had time to bone up. She bought a couple more history books of the period: she had a sizeable collection by now. There was nothing about those casket letters she didn't know – forgeries, planted by spies and enemies. She remembered with anguish the murder of her Italian secretary, clever David Rizzio, though she had mixed feelings about her useless husband Darnley being found dead in the garden after they blew up his house, the poxy shit. Not that she'd known about the explosion plans in advance. Naughty Bothwell!

She was looking forward.

However, she gathered from the tone of Sal's emails that Sal wasn't as keen on Marla's visit as she'd been at first. Tough, thought Marla. I'm not turning down my chance to see the old stomping grounds once again.

*

Sal met her at the airport. At first Marla didn't recognise her: she was thinner, and she'd had her hair changed – she was a strawberry blonde now. She'd definitely had something done to her nose, and her chubby underchin was gone, and her teeth were whiter. Her make-up was laid on with a trowel. Marla knew the clothes were expensive, but she couldn't tell how expensive: they were well beyond Marla's range. The total effect was striking. Not what you'd call beautiful, thought Marla grudgingly, but striking. Beyond a doubt. You had to look at Sal twice, as you'd look at a parade.

Sal gave Marla a hug, teetering forward on her massively high heels, and said coolly how nice it was that Marla could visit. 'The Earl's in the car,' she said as they walked towards the exit. 'You'll like him, he's a sweetie!'

'The Earl?' said Marla.

'Of Essex,' said Sal.

Marla stopped. 'The Earl of Essex?'

'In a past life,' said Sal. 'His name's Dave, in the present. Dave McLeod.'

'What are you doing with the Earl of Essex?' she asked. 'Which Earl of Essex?' She was getting a bad feeling.

'Well, as Elizabeth the First,' said Sal, 'I feel I owe it to him. To make it turn out better this time around. After all, I did sign his death warrant, although I loved him passionately. But what choice did I have?'

'Just a minute,' said Marla. 'You're not Elizabeth the First. You're Cleopatra!'

'Oh, Marla,' said Sal. 'That was then!' She laughed. 'You can have more than one! It's a game! Anyway, we're cousins now!' She linked her arm through Marla's. 'Cousin Mary! Too bad we never met, in the old days. But carpe diem!'

Evil witch, thought Marla. I was innocent, but you had me killed for treason. Then you tried to get out of it by saying you'd been fooled. She had a vivid memory of the humiliation she'd felt when her red wig had come off as the executioner hoisted her severed head. And then her dog had run in under her skirts. What a farce.

Dave, the Earl of Essex, was a red-faced, white-haired Scotsman who'd been in the construction business. He was older than Bob/Marc had been, and Marla was willing to bet he was richer. He pried himself up and out of the car to shake Marla's hand.

'She's my little Gloriana,' he chortled, patting Sal on her designer bum, winking at Marla. 'And I take it you're our long-lost Mary!'

Watch your back, Marla wanted to tell him. Don't drink any syllabubs. Don't go on any barges.

*

Sal was no longer in mourning for Bob/Marc. In fact she barely mentioned him, apart from saying that this particular segment of her past had now been 'resolved'. Her main object in having Marla visit appeared to be showing off. Her house was vast, and so were the grounds around it, and so was the garage in which she kept her several Mercedes, and so were the closets in which she stored her extensive wardrobe: there was a special walk-in for her shoe collection. She had a lot of jewellery, as well. Just like Elizabeth the First, thought Marla: her clothes were always better than mine, even before she was keeping me cooped up in those draughty, damp castles, with nothing at all to spend on decent cloaks. So cheap of her. Vindictive. Jealous of my charisma. Dancing around in luxury, while I sat embroidering elephants. Neglected. Laughed at. So unfair.

The next day Essex/Dave was visiting his grandchildren in Stirling and getting together with a friend, one of the many William Wallaces; so, after her hair appointment in the morning and an argument with her crabby Scottish gardener, Sal took Marla to see Holyroodhouse.

'Don't be too disappointed,' she said. 'It's a bit of a tourist trap. It won't be what you remember.'

Marla thought the building looked vaguely familiar, but she'd seen a lot of pictures of it. So much is since my time, thought Marla. It's too clean. We never used to bother much with that. She didn't like the long gallery, with all those portraits of Stewarts – going back to Adam to show how noble they were, said Sal with a dismissive laugh – and all with the same big noses. Whoever'd done the arms hadn't been paying much attention: if extended, some of those arms would dangle down to below the knees.

Her own portrait was awful – not pretty at all. But everyone had raved about her beauty, back then. Men had strewn themselves. She remembered Bothwell, his burning eyes, his kidnapper's passion . . . it ended badly though. And he could have done with a toothbrush, thought Marla in her present mode. We all could, back then.

'There's some resemblance, don't you think?' said Sal. 'You know, you should try auburn, for your hair. That would bring it out more.'

They went through more rooms, Sal's heels clacking annoyingly. Not too sensible for sightseeing, thought Marla. Purple. Jimmy Choos, as Sal had pointed out.

They went upstairs. They saw more furniture. They looked at pictures. Marla kept waiting for a frisson of recognition – something she'd known, something that was hers – but there was nothing. It was as if she'd never lived there.

'Here's the bedchamber,' said Sal. 'And the famous supper room.' She was watching Marla, with a little smirk. 'Where Rizzio was murdered,' she added. 'Your so-called private secretary.'

'I know,' said Marla. Now she really did feel something. Panic, despair . . . she'd screamed a lot. They'd held a gun on her, while poor David . . . He'd hidden behind her, but they'd dragged him out. There were tears in her eyes now. What if it was all true, and she'd really been there somehow?

No. Surely not.

'They used to do the pretend blood with red paint,' said Sal, laughing a little. 'But people kept chipping it off, and anyway it looked so fake. It's much better now, with brown varnish. See, over here.'

Sure enough, there on the wooden floor were some realistic-looking stains. On the wall beside them was a plaque – not claiming exactly that the varnish was Rizzio's actual blood, but pointing out that this was the spot where he'd been stabbed fifty-six times and then thrown down the stairs.

And those were the very stairs. Marla was shivering now. It had been a terrible shock, and her six months pregnant. She could have lost the baby. They'd taken off David's lovely clothes, like the robbers they were. And his jewels. Stuck him naked in a hole in the ground.

'Tell me,' said Sal. 'Was it true? That you were sleeping with him? That ugly little music master?' She seemed not to notice Marla's tears.

Marla got control of herself. 'How could you even think that?' she said. 'I was the Queen!' Now she felt anger. But she kept her voice low: there were some American tourists over by the four-poster bed, examining the embroidered hangings.

'A lot of people thought it,' said Sal teasingly. 'You were really hot, back then. You didn't exactly restrain yourself. The French Dauphin, then Darnley, then Bothwell, and who knows who else? So why not Rizzio?'

'He was gay,' said Marla faintly, but Sal went right on.

'They said you were quite the slut. You should get into that mode again, have some fun for a change. If you lost a few pounds . . .'

'You put them up to it,' said Marla. Had she read that somewhere? She felt her hands clenching into fists. 'You paid them! Those conspirators! You wanted me dead, so you could have everything!' Queen bee, she thought. Her and her shoe collection, and her fucking fraudulent rich old Earl of Essex. And her fleet of Mercedes. She took a step towards Sal. Sal took a step backwards, wobbling on her high heels. Now her back was to the stairwell.

'Marla, Marla,' she said nervously. 'Don't get carried away! It's a game!'

Not a game, thought Marla. She didn't consciously mean to push so hard. Sal went over backwards, down the stairs. There was a screech, and an unpleasant crack. Tit for tat, thought Marla.

'It was the shoes,' she said afterwards. She was sobbing

uncontrollably by then. 'She turned her ankle. She shouldn't have been wearing them, not for sightseeing. I told her!'

★

The Earl of Essex was dismayed at first, but Marla helped him through the mourning period. 'Poor Gloriana,' he said at last. 'It was vanity killed her. She was always too stuck on herself, don't you think?'

Then he confessed that, like so many men, he'd secretly fancied Mary all along. Although he'd never met her in the flesh. Until now.

There Goes Me

ISLA DEWAR

As soon as he stepped into the office, Callum knew somebody had been in there. He stood, sniffed. The place always smelled musty, a touch of damp. But today there was a slight undertow scent. Calvin Klein. Mrs Dancer's file was missing. He'd left it on his desk, pen perfectly placed alongside it. He felt sick, a rumbling of nerves through his stomach. Someone had been in here, in his space, breathing his air. He hated that. He'd have to wipe the doorknob and the window where they'd got in. Germs.

He ran his fingers through his hair, then went through to the small loo and washed his hands.

Was this how people felt when they discovered someone had entered their home and taken their stuff? He felt a flush of shame. For that's what he'd done. Often.

He stole things. He'd taken it up when he was eight, and stopped eight years ago, when he was thirty-two. It was his secret, he told nobody about his murky past. Well, he wouldn't have been able to cope with some people's liberal understanding of other people's social failings and disgraces.

He could imagine Fran's take on the situation. 'Perhaps you were an unhappy child,' she'd say. No, he'd been happy. His childhood plates had overflowed with puddings. He'd been given a bike for Christmas and a leather jacket for his fourteenth birthday. His parents were wonderful. He was a rogue.

She might suggest a visit to a psychiatrist. A nurse, she believed in all things medical. She thought psychiatry an emotional antibiotic. It zapped phobias and troublesome memories.

Callum didn't think so. He wasn't keen on analysis. He knew too many nasty things about himself already, without discovering more. Once, his handwriting had been analysed. The results, horribly accurate, had shocked him. But really, stealing had been his pleasure. Now his pleasure was eating.

Up till that moment of stepping into the office and realising somebody had been here, today had been a good day. And February rarely offered many of them. Seagulls yammering in from the beach had woken him, such alarmist birds. He'd reached across the bed for Fran, but she wasn't there. Half past nine, she'd be off to work, taking the car.

Walking along the prom to his office at the end of Portobello High Street he hadn't seen many slippery faces. A thin winter sun was shining, small glimmers of light on the water. This was his patch, backdrop to his childhood picnics on the sands: ham and lettuce sandwiches with salad cream – it was years before his mother discovered mayo – toffee Yo-Yos and Vimto. God, he'd loved that food. Now, of course, he'd hate it. Sometimes, sophistication was a curse.

He'd whiled away teenage nights hanging about the funfair, longing to be one of the boys in cowboy boots and leather jackets who hung about the shooting range. Nostalgia for him was loud music, lights, screams from people on the rides and the smell of hotdogs and burgers lingering in his nostrils. In his twenties he'd moved to

Leith, but he'd returned to move in with Fran in her flat in King's Place, six months after meeting her.

He had his day's list in his head. Go see Mrs Wolski, shop for food. But first, finish report for Mrs Lego Hair (real name Cynthia Jackson). She'd asked him to compile a case against her neighbour Mrs Dancer (Flora Drummond). He gave the clients he didn't like nicknames. He hated this kind of work, but needed the money. The business was failing. He'd not long filled in his tax return and this year had barely cleared ten grand.

'How're things going?' Fran had asked.

'Very well, I've expanded.' Lie, lie, lie, that's the thing to do.

'Into what?'

'Domestic cases, stuff like that.' Once you've started lying, stick with it. Lie till your jaw hurts and your eyes ache from keeping contact with the eyes of the person you're lying to. Then, when you're done lying, wash your hands.

Mrs Lego Hair claimed Mrs Dancer held wild parties, sold drugs from her home, bought alcohol for local kids. Her words had spilled out, a storm of accusation, and barely a breath drawn. The woman had been furious. Such hate, it made Callum recoil. She wanted a report to give to Mrs Dancer's landlord. She wanted the woman evicted. 'I want her and her brats out of here. I don't want my children exposed to that kind of behaviour.'

She had an organised hairdo, like the stiff bob that clipped on to the heads of the little plastic Lego figures. She had three organised children. Callum had noticed their schedule pinned by a pineapple magnet to the fridge – cello lessons, tennis, swimming, piano, drama classes. Lives stuffed with good intentions, and not a moment's boredom allowed. These kids would leave home, discover the glories of hanging about, and go berserk idling.

Mrs Dancer's children weren't brats. The younger one, the Frolicker, skipped by her mother's side when they set out for school in the morning; the older daughter, the Carer, walked a few paces behind. A worrier, this one, small furrowed brow, she was nine or ten going on fifty. They were both immaculately turned out.

Callum had no doubts Mrs Dancer was dealing. He knew the faces that visited her house, slippery all of them. They were people he'd met in pubs, pawnshops or on the street in the days when he lived in one room in a building off Junction Street and got by on small pickings from breaking and entering – jewellery, cash, books, CDs and food. He'd loved raiding fridges. Taking food was an excellent ploy. You never knew what you'd find; also, it saved you the bother of shopping.

He'd regularly seen Flaky, whose real name he didn't know. In fact, Flaky was so flaky he probably didn't remember his real name. Flaky, because he spoke rubbish – started talking about one thing then drifted off talking about something else; often he walked off halfway through a conversation, forgetting what he'd been talking about. And Flaky because of his skin condition, which wasn't very nice, Callum thought. Not that Flaky minded. Perhaps he didn't notice or care what he was called. Callum would have minded being named after his condition. Obsessive-compulsive disorder was a bit of a mouthful.

He was getting better. It had been a long time since he'd had to get out of bed to fix his shoes because they weren't lined up properly. He no longer tried to count his words as he spoke. He still liked his beer cans to be in regimental order in the fridge, though. When he had six cans, he had to drink two so he'd be left with four. He hated odd numbers. But he had managed to cut down on the hand washing. He didn't do it twenty times a day. It was eight or ten now. He still counted.

Last night, he'd parked across from Mrs Dancer's house in Dalkeith Street and photographed her callers. Flaky had been among them, but Callum hadn't snapped him. You kept your friends out of things. After all, you never knew when you'd need them.

To keep himself going, Callum had a box of sandwiches, two apples, a flask of coffee and a pack of chocolate digestives. Well, it was going to be a long night. He listened to the radio because the only tape on the deck had been Fran's Leonard Cohen. At eleven o'clock, or thereabouts, he'd fallen asleep. He'd woken two hours later, shivering, neck cricked and face pressed against the side window. He thought he'd been drooling.

There was a red Beetle convertible parked at Mrs Dancer's door. Very conspicuous. 'Don't be conspicuous,' the Flake had said in the days before his brain melted. 'Keep it dull on the outside.' Mrs Dancer and a friend were dancing on the lawn.

Callum thought, there goes me. He'd lived on a twenty-four-year high. He'd thought he was living on his wits. He'd stolen a little bit here and a little bit there and hadn't needed to do the nine to five.

He hadn't danced on lawns, he hadn't done drugs – well,

nothing heavy anyway. But, just like Mrs Dancer, he'd thought he had his life sussed. She would think her neighbours boring straights. She'd imagine she was wild, free.

He photographed her, twirling barefoot in the frost in her tangled garden, wearing a thin slip of a red dress, the Frolicker balanced on her hip. The house was lit up, every light burning, old Rod Stewart hits blaring out from open windows. Do Ya Think I'm Sexy?

The Carer, pale and anxious, was watching at the front door. He guessed the Dancer was hot. Heroin sometimes did that. Drug-heated body oblivious to the sub-zero temperatures. She and her friend, an air hostess – she was in her uniform – were laughing. Something was pleasing them. He guessed the neighbours wouldn't be sharing her glee.

When the friend got into her car and squealed off into the night, Callum followed. The streets were never quite empty. Always somebody about, and Princes Street never stopped. He often wondered what the people he saw were up to. Revellers perhaps, or thieves, like he'd once been. Not that he worked nights. He preferred afternoons.

You could get a good look about in daylight. That had been a joy, poking around other people's houses. He'd always been nosey. He would thumb through photograph albums, read mail, look at postcards, scan bookshelves, criticise CD collections.

If only he hadn't started writing notes to his victims, or benefactors, as he called them. That had almost been his downfall. *This kitchen is messy*, he'd told one household. *Your diet lacks fibre*, to another. *I hate your décor, Wash your salad box, You've got naughty photographs, There's no love here*. He knew secrets, things people hid, things people did. Houses had specific smells and atmospheres; you could breathe in the personalities of the people who lived in them. He'd loved being a thief.

The air hostess parked in Cumberland Street, disappeared into a basement flat. Callum double-parked, slipped over to her front door and noted her name. He wouldn't put it in his report. What was it to Mrs Lego Hair where Mrs Dancer got her stuff?

A blue Renault pulled out at the same time as he did. It followed him to the end of the street, and when he hit London Road, it was still behind him. He stopped in Portobello High Street, watched it go past. Waited. Then turned back and went home. Nobody followed. But then whoever was in the blue Renault had his number plate, which was registered to his office. A couple of phone calls and they'd know where he worked, what he did and the colour of his underpants. It was a worry.

Now, in his office, recovering from the shock of the break-in, he checked his phone messages, none, his emails, none, deleted all his spam, quite a lot, then got Mrs Lego Hair's report up on his screen, added his new information, and was printing it out again when a small woman, in her seventies Callum guessed, stuck her head round the door. She wore a long red raincoat, and carried a bulging canvas Porty Shopper bag with several leeks drooping over the top. 'Mr Watson?'

'Yes.'

'I need your services.'

He told her she needed to make an appointment. She

said she didn't see why, since he was sitting there looking at a printer and obviously not doing any real detecting work, and she was here already, so why make an appointment? 'I need you to find my cat.'

He said he didn't do cats, or indeed any pets. 'There are specialist firms that do, though.'

'Probably. But you're local. So you can keep your eye out for Humphrey when you're out and about. He's grey, two years old, blue collar with bell, neutered, likes rabbit in gravy cat food.'

'And you are?'

'Mrs McGhee, Janice. I live in John Street and my cat had been missing for two weeks.'

Callum drummed his fingers on his desk. Thought about this and said, 'OK. I'll keep my eye out.' Anything to get rid of her.

'There you go,' she said. 'How long did that take? Five minutes? There's no need for an appointment.' She picked up her Porty Shopper bag and left.

Callum wasn't awfully keen on cats. Dogs, he liked. Though in his thieving days he'd avoided the homes of dog owners. Unless it was golden retrievers, who seemed to greet everybody, even burglars, with thumping tails.

In his old life, he'd hung out in pubs in Leith and the Grassmarket with out-of-work musicians and people who hadn't seen the point of having a job. They might have been called slackers, but they were all too scruffy even for that. He'd told his parents he was in a band, The Sadly Decaying, with his mates, Scott McGregor and Bradley Foster. Scott had disappeared to live in a hut on Skye.

Bradley had inherited money, and had become rich enough to enter elite circles and schmooze people better connected than a dishevelled ne'er-do-well like Callum. He'd met, and married, Trudy Bryce, who had a chain of restaurants and delicatessens across the city. Trudy was a woman often seen in magazine style pages – groomed, elegant, poised, perfect nails. She claimed to have an instinct for handbags. Always had the *It* bag before anyone else, but had always stopped carrying it as soon as it became popular. 'A woman has to be ahead of the crowd,' she said. She was master of the dismissive eyeflick. And, before introducing him to any of her friends, she made sure Bradley had several Hugo Boss suits, a decent haircut, a dusting of a tan and a respectable job. He'd gone into property.

Flaky had instructed Callum in the fine art of breaking and entering. 'Don't get greedy. In and out, take what you can carry. Try to be inconspicuous.' Flaky wore a bright red T-shirt, a tweed jacket with patched elbows, jeans, a hat with a feather in the band and sunglasses. He only advised being inconspicuous.

They'd been walking along George Street when Flaky had spotted an unchained bike and casually wheeled it off. 'A financial investment opportunity,' he'd said.

Back then, everybody used the term. Callum supposed they'd picked it up from the money pages of the newspapers they read on their long cider-fuelled afternoons, lounging in pubs listening to the Happy Mondays and The Stone Roses, rating films on their sex scenes and competing to find who could stuff the most mini Scotch eggs into their mouth.

He'd worked alone. Flaky had become too flaky to trust. He cycled everywhere. Broke into houses in Colinton, Morningside, Corstorphine, the Meadows – never forage near home. He never worked Portobello where his parents lived.

An accurate description of him appeared in the *Evening News*: *Early thirties, about five feet nine inches tall, brown curly hair, wears jeans, white T-shirt and long black raincoat, rides a silver mountain bike, carries an old game bag*. They'd got an expert to analyse some of his notes – *Solitary, sensual, indulgent, a procrastinator, a coward, makes lists. The notes are always four words long; this man avoids odd numbers, suggesting obsessive-compulsive disorder.*

He remembered well his mother sitting at the kitchen table reading it. 'Why, Callum,' she'd said, 'that's just like you.' That was why he'd given up. Oh, he didn't fancy getting arrested, charged, appearing in court and being jailed. But mostly, he hadn't wanted to see his mother's face when she found out what he'd been up to.

He put Mrs Lego Hair's report into a folder, enclosed her bill. Then sat, drumming the desk with his fingers. Perhaps he should phone Mrs Dancer, warn her she might be in danger. Someone with nasty intentions, who knew what she was up to, had her address. They might pay a visit. He sniffed; leave it till later. He'd drop in and talk to her after he'd delivered the report. He was indeed a procrastinator.

Life in the straight lane hadn't been easy. Thirty-two with no qualifications, no work record and no CV, he'd found a job in a record exchange on Leith Walk. It suited him.

He didn't have to dress up, music played all day, and Valvona & Crolla was just a step away.

Then he'd met Fran at a party. He shied away from words like love. All he knew was that whenever he saw her walking towards him something strange happened inside. Heart skipping a beat? And his face took on a life of its own, did what it wanted to do. It smiled.

Walking along busy streets he'd put his arm round her. 'Watch out for slippery faces.'

'Watch out for what?'

'Slippery faces. Faces among the sea of faces that belong to people who are looking for a swift financial investment opportunity, who do not have good intentions.'

Fran had told her father, Phillip O'Brien, an ex-police sergeant who now ran a small private investigation agency specialising in corporate insurance and some divorces.

Phillip had asked to meet Callum, and had been impressed by his understanding of the criminal mind. Callum shrugged, he read a lot, he said. After many Sunday lunches and chats in the pub, Phillip had offered Callum a job doing the legwork for his agency as he was no longer up to it.

Phillip died three years ago, leaving the business to his daughter, which meant that, technically, Fran was Callum's boss as well as his partner. Not that she took much interest, she left it all to him.

It had been downhill all the way, really. Fran said it was because he looked scruffy. 'Get a suit, wear a tie. You don't look trustworthy.' He thought he shouldn't look trustworthy, because he wasn't.

*

In the afternoon, he went to see Mrs Wolski in her bungalow in Stapeley Avenue. It was unassuming, ordinary. Neat lawns, clipped hedge, pruned rose bushes – things that said, Respectable People Live Here.

He liked her house, wouldn't have left a note if he'd come here in his naughty youth. The walls were pale, covered in paintings, the floor polished – old wood – rugs scattered here and there. She told him to call her Lily, showed him into the living room. 'Sit by the fire. I'll get you a cup of tea. I've made scones.' He didn't take a seat, he wandered the walls. He didn't know much about art, but he knew expensive when he saw it. God, even the frames were classy.

He'd never stolen pictures. He hadn't any contacts in the art world. He'd been mocked in the press when he'd broken into a house that backed onto Corstorphine Hill and helped himself to fifty pounds in cash, a fake Gucci watch, half a dozen CDs and a free range chicken from the fridge, and had left a small Constable original.

By this time, he was making a name for himself. Somebody had told the press about the housebreaker who left comments on his victims' lifestyles and had sometimes tidied up their kitchens. The *Evening News* had called him the Gay Gourmet Thief after the old joke about gay burglars who didn't take anything but rearranged the furniture.

Gay Gourmet Thief strikes again, and this time he misses a priceless painting while helping himself to a chicken from the fridge.

Two days later there had been another short paragraph about him: *Gay Gourmet returns to house and steals Constable painting.*

He'd considered writing to the editor pointing out that 1. He was not gay, and 2. He'd seen the painting, a watercolour of cows in a meadow, but didn't take it. It was too traceable. Nobody could trace a Sainsbury's free range chicken, especially after it had been roasted with garlic and tarragon. And eaten. 3. He hadn't returned to the house and stolen the painting.

'Looking at the collection?' said Lily. She put a tray on the coffee table, poured two cups of tea and told Callum to help himself to a scone. 'Used to bake every day. But it's not the same with Max not here.'

He nodded. He asked if Lily had informed the police about her missing husband.

'No police.' She waved her hands in dismay at the idea.

He looked round at the artwork on the walls.

'Not what you'd expect to find in an ordinary shopkeeper's bungalow in Portobello. They'd ask questions,' said Lily.

'You cooked the books?'

She wouldn't answer that. 'Ask no questions, hear no lies. You have to find my husband. He's old.'

Callum asked if Max had taken his passport.

'No. He's here.'

'Here?'

'Not far away. I can feel him. He's watching me. He sent me a Valentine card.' She took it down from the mantelpiece and gave it to him. 'He did it himself. It's a copy of the painting he gave me for our fortieth wedding anniversary.'

'A Constable,' said Callum.

'You know your art.'

He shook his head. 'No. I just know this piece of art.' He'd seen it in a house that backed onto Corstorphine Hill. He took another scone. 'These are very good.'

She agreed, 'It's the buttermilk.'

He asked about Max's habits. Did he have many friends? Where were his haunts? Had he done this before? Could he, perhaps, be having an affair?

'Good heavens, no. He's too old for that. No haunts, just work then home. Not many friends. Habits? Into the shop at seven, open till six thirty at night. Home, supper, television, a glass of malt then bed. On Tuesdays, Wednesdays and Thursdays he collected his specialities. He'd go off at eleven in the morning and come back about two. We live very regular lives.'

How Callum loved the specialities. The shop, in Bath Street, was small. For years it had been the place people went for odds and ends – milk, sugar, a packet of tea. Supermarkets had almost seen it off. Then the specialities started to appear. There had been extra virgin olive oils, artichoke hearts, anchovies packed in salt, jars of pimentos, specialist vinegars, vintage wines and much more. All at knock down prices. It had been Portobello's secret. Nobody whispered about the place because they didn't want anybody to find out where you could buy a twenty-year-old Burgundy for a tenner. Callum was a keen customer.

He asked Lily for a photo of Max and had a look round his study. Nothing much, no emails on his ancient computer, no nasty letters, nothing to indicate that here was a man about to make an exit from his life. He leafed through the accounts book. The shop was doing almost as badly as he was. There was no mention anywhere of the specialities.

As he left he asked if he could borrow the Constable for a couple of days. Something he had to check out. Lily reluctantly put it into a plastic bag, peered at him over her specs, an imperious look. 'Take care of it. It's precious.'

He took the number twelve bus into Leith, and called on his old friend, the lager-and-loafer man turned tanned, honed Bradley Foster. The man who had more than just made-to-measure suits: his tasteful, demanding wife had ensured he had a complete bespoke life.

Once, Bradley had made a small living shoplifting at Marks & Spencer's and Currys. He took people's lists near the front door, shoplifted the items and, for a fee, delivered them to the customer outside. As a financial investment opportunity, Callum found this too risky.

After Bradley had been left what the Flake called a tasty amount of money he'd gone into property development, buying broken down homes cheaply, doing them up cheaply, and selling them as expensively as he could. He also had shares in his wife's restaurant and delicatessen business. His offices overlooked the Royal Yacht. He collected art, a passion more than a hobby.

Still, he was always glad to see his old mate. He found it gratifying to catch up with someone who wasn't doing as well as he was.

'How's it going, Callum?' Looking pointedly at Callum's thickening waist – his shirt, black no tie, was spilling over the top of his jeans.

'Fine.'

He snorted, 'You, a private investigator. Poacher turned gamekeeper, eh?' He always said this. And he always snorted.

Callum shrugged, 'Who'd have thought it.' He always shrugged.

He slid the Constable across a vast shiny expanse of desk. 'What do you think of this?'

Bradley picked it up, stared at it, held it under his desk lamp then took it across to the window. 'It's a forgery.'

'Is it?'

'Yes. Where did you get it?'

'A client.'

'This is a copy of a painting that was stolen years ago from a house in Corstorphine. I always thought you did it.'

Callum said art was not his style.

'It's not unusual for forgeries of stolen art to turn up. Max Wolski bought it at auction, cost him forty quid. I was there. Is he your client?'

Callum told him no. He thanked Bradley for his time and made for the door.

Bradley said, 'I hate thieves.'

Callum turned, 'Then you must hate me. You must hate yourself.'

'I do,' said Bradley. 'I hate what I did, and who I was. But I've given up. I find it's like giving up smoking, you come to hate the smell of it.'

Back at his office, Callum collected the report for Mrs Lego Hair and locked the painting in his desk drawer. He'd return it tomorrow. He made his evening list: go home, make supper, wash up, deliver report and bill to Mrs Lego Hair, warn Mrs Dancer, go to pub.

He was striding along the prom, thinking that, despite the break-in, today had been a good day, when he saw the cat. It was grey, no collar, but that could easily have been lost. He couldn't tell if it had been neutered and had no intention of checking to find out. But it certainly looked like Humphrey to him. It was hunched, like an unhappy hen, at the foot of Bath Street. When he scooped it up, it yowled in fury, lacerated his hand. He shoved the animal inside his jacket, and carried it, howling in protest, back to John Street. He rang Mrs McGhee's doorbell, thinking, nice one. Job done. She might even pay me in cash, a quick fifty quid.

Mrs McGhee opened the door, saw the wriggling cat, ears flat and hissing, and the faint flicker of a smile crossed her face. She looked closer. 'That's not Humphrey.'

Callum said, 'Oh.'

'Poor wee thing,' said Mrs McGhee. 'Give him here.'

The cat calmed as soon as she took him to her. 'Poor wee thing.' She stroked it, 'I bet you're hungry.' Then to Callum, 'It's half starved and flea-bitten. And it's not Humphrey.' She took the cat inside, and shut the door.

Callum started back home, scratching himself, worrying about fleas and, sucking his wounded hand, rabies. He made a new evening list: home, shower, TCP on hand, supper, washing up, bill to Mrs Lego Hair, warn Mrs Dancer, Ormelie for a drink, then home, another shower, more TCP. You couldn't be too careful.

Fran went with him to deliver the report; she fancied he owed her a pint for forgetting Valentine's Day. Even before they turned into the street, they heard the noise. Elvis Presley. The curtains were drawn tight, front doors locked, on every house but one. Mrs Dancer's was ablaze. A funfair, Callum thought, music roaring, everything adazzle and the front door wide open. 'It'd be better if it was Elvis's early period,' he said to Fran. 'I always hated that Vegas stuff.'

And Fran said, 'There's a wee girl in the garden.' She ran across, crouched in front of the Frolicker. 'Are you all right?'

The child didn't answer, she looked towards the house. Fran picked her up and went in. Callum behind her. The place smelled sweet, herby, boozy, and there was the thick, almost metallic tang of blood.

Mrs Dancer was in the living room, lying in a swirl of smashed miniature bottles, TV set, hi-fi and blood. The room had been destroyed. Mrs Dancer's face had been slashed from forehead to chin, blood everywhere. She looked to have lost an eye. Both her knees were smashed. Bruises down both arms. A baseball bat, Callum thought. Her skull looked crushed. She couldn't call out, or scream. Someone had tied her hands behind her back and stuffed a pair of knickers into her mouth.

Fran removed them, put her fingers to Mrs Dancer's throat. 'She's alive, call an ambulance.' She turned to Callum. He wasn't there. He was outside throwing up.

Fran dialled 999, fetched towels, staunched the bleeding. She found the Carer in the living room hiding behind the sofa, led her into the kitchen with her younger sister, sat them at the table, said soothing words, then went back to see what she could do for Mrs Dancer.

Callum heaved and spat, then retched some more.

Blood and gore always made him heave. He could hear sirens, see the blue lights sparking in the distance.

Mrs Dancer was whisked away, whimpering, wrapped in blankets, oxygen mask on her face. The children were removed from the scene; they'd be questioned later but the detective inspector doubted the younger one would be able to speak for quite a while. He'd seen it before – 'Mute, trauma does that.' He took Callum's name and address, and asked what he was doing here.

Callum had been going to say he was just passing but Fran chipped in, 'Delivering a report to the woman next door.'

'What kind of report?'

'She asked me to collect evidence on the woman who lives here. She thought she was dealing in drugs.' He took out his licence and his card. He was proud of his licence, had studied Scottish and English law and sat his ABI exams to get it.

The detective handed it back. 'You knew she was dealing and you didn't inform the police?'

'I only knew for sure last night.'

'If you'd told us we might have prevented this happening.'

He told them about the air hostess in Cumberland Street. He didn't mention the blue Renault or the break-in at his office. Guilt. He'd been the one who led the people who'd beaten up Mrs Dancer to her. He was giving himself enough of a ticking off without getting a more serious one from the police. Or worse, Fran. He handed over his report and agreed to visit the station tomorrow to give a statement.

He and Fran walked home. They didn't speak till Fran

said, 'You're useless. Throwing up.' She often told him he was useless, but this was different. She meant it.

He said he'd long suspected he was useless.

Next morning, he lingered under the duvet, making his list. Take the Constable back to Mrs Wolski, give police statement, then back to the office, print out another report and bill for Mrs Lego Hair. It was raining.

He delivered the painting, then went to the police station in the High Street at two o'clock. Mrs Dancer was in intensive care and probably wouldn't be able to talk for a few days. They thought she'd been undercutting other dealers. 'We got quite a haul in her house,' the DI said. 'Ecstasy, cannabis, heroin, all in Tupperware boxes.' The Frolicker was still mute.

The detective inspector gave him a cup of tea, and told him they'd been to see Mrs Jackson. Callum got the impression he didn't like Mrs Lego Hair either.

The air hostess had been stopped coming off a flight from Amsterdam. She'd had quite a stash of cannabis in her bag and was in custody, but safe.

He walked back along the High Street, printed out Mrs Lego Hair's report for the third time. He went home, walking along the prom as usual.

The second grey cat was down on the sands, looking more miserable than the first. Grey cats, they were everywhere. Once you started looking, there were hundreds of them. He hadn't noticed this before. The tide was coming in, it was mewling. Callum clambered through the railings, jumped down, stumbled over the sand and picked up the cat. It purred. This was surely Humphrey.

He went back along the prom, up John Street, rang Mrs McGhee's doorbell. When she opened the door, he held out the cat in triumph. 'Humphrey, I think.'

'No.'

He turned to go, planning to put the cat back where he found it. But Mrs McGhee said, 'Oh, give it here.'

She took it in, and as Callum walked down the path, shouted, 'Don't come back here. Don't bring me any more cats. You're bloody useless.'

He said someone had already mentioned that to him.

Home, he showered, worrying about more fleas. He picked up the car and drove to deliver Mrs Lego Hair's bill. The house next door was still cordoned off.

Mrs Lego Hair didn't invite him in, waved the report away. 'I don't need it. The woman's gone. And the police have been here taking a statement. They got my name from you. I thought people like you didn't divulge clients' names.'

Callum said he could hardly keep her out of this since he'd been at the scene of the crime when the police arrived. Meantime, he'd carried out the investigative work he'd been asked to do, and here was the bill.

'Bill?' said Mrs Lego Hair. 'You set the police on me and you give me a bill?' She launched into a rant that included her children being witness to horrific goings-on, the damage to her reputation from having the police come to her door, and the effect of this sort of disgusting thing on local house prices. 'Bill?' she said again. 'I don't think so.' She shut the door.

He was driving home, heading for King's Place, when

he saw Max trudging towards Stapeley Avenue. He stopped the car, got out. 'Max?'

The old man stopped, turned and smiled. 'Just going home.' He knew Callum, a regular customer.

Callum offered him a lift, 'It's freezing out here.' Then, 'Your wife's got me looking for you.'

Max sighed, got into the car, shivered at the sudden heat. 'It's cold.'

Callum asked where he'd been.

'At home. In the garage. Wandering about town all day, sleeping in my car. Edinburgh's a lovely place, you know.'

Callum knew.

'Couldn't count the times people came up to me, asked if I was all right. Didn't get mugged, didn't get my pocket picked, wasn't urged to join the Moonies. Walked Princes Street, and down to Stockbridge. There are some lovely places to get coffee.'

Callum agreed. 'Didn't Lily hear you in the garage?'

'Takes a sleeping pill and she's dead to the world.' He turned to Callum, 'Couldn't face her. Couldn't tell her. I've lost bloody everything.' He slumped. 'Such a bloody good scheme I had.'

'The specialities?' said Callum.

'Exactly. We were going broke. So I started the specialities. Olive oil, anchovies, nice wines – weekend treats. I acquired them.'

'Financial investment opportunities?'

'Nice way to put it. Went out round all the delis in Edinburgh, a little bit here, a little bit there. Nobody knew. Sold everything cut price.'

Callum said, 'Nice one.' He liked a good scheme.

'There they were on their stand, *Weekend Treats, A Tenner and Under.*'

Callum knew.

'And I kept it small. There were never more than thirty offers. That's enough to acquire. When the money mounted up, I bought paintings, which I sold. Had receipts. Been doing it for forty years. Acquiring specialities, buying and selling art. I was a millionaire.'

Callum thought, there goes me. Someone with a nice little scheme. I slipped into houses, took a little of this and a little of that. People didn't even know I'd been there. Who'd notice a CD missing? They'd think they'd mislaid it. A pack of chicken fillets? They'd think they hadn't picked it up from the checkout counter. A few quid? They'd think they'd spent it on something and forgotten. But, I just had to write the notes. I had to let the world know how clever I was.

'Well,' said Max. 'What do you want when you've made a million?'

Dreams of wealth drifted into Callum's mind – a swimming pool, a top of the range sound system, a huge fridge, a Porsche.

Max said, 'You want another million.'

The thought hadn't occurred to Callum.

'So, I met a chap at an art auction. Property developer. He told me he was building a holiday resort in Spain. I invested. Three weeks ago I find out the company's gone bust. I've lost everything. Everything. Money in the bank, my paintings and my house. You tell me, how do you tell that to your wife? It's not that I'm scared of her. I'm ashamed of me.'

Callum said, 'The property developer. It wasn't Bradley Foster, was it?'

'The very man. Nice chap.'

They drew up at Max's house. Callum steadied him as he shuffled up the drive. The man was light as air, old bones, tired skin. He was weeping.

Callum rang the bell. He thought he'd be in for a small bit of glory. Some praise; he'd found the missing man. But Lily hardly noticed him.

She spread her arms, took Max to her, and cried. She led him inside, thanked Callum and shut the door.

You didn't have to be Einstein to figure it out. Max had been helping himself to specialities from Bradley's wife's shops. It was like old smoke, Bradley hated the smell of thieves. He'd offered the old man a chance to make a swift killing, then he'd pulled the rug from under him. Killed the deal, leaving Max with nothing. It was revenge: you don't steal from me. It was shitty, Callum thought.

Max would soon be free of it all, though. Callum had seen it before. That wheeze, that grey pallor, that resigned walk. It didn't do to live in your car when you were seventy-five. The man had given up.

He lasted a fortnight, then pneumonia took him. It was in the deaths column in the *Evening News.*

Meantime, Callum had a new case, a woman who thought her husband had a second family on the other side of town. So it was some time before he dropped in on Lily.

She sat him by the fire, brought him tea, and noticed him noticing the empty walls. 'All sold, I'm afraid. A Bradley Foster phoned with an offer. He bought the lot, including the Constable. The house will have to go too. I'll fetch up in a home staring at the wall while some hideous young people try to get me to join in a singsong. 'Yellow Submarine', I hate that song. And I'm afraid I can't pay you for your work.'

Callum said not to worry about it. He knew of a painting in a house that backed onto Corstorphine Hill that might just solve the problem, but he didn't mention this to Lily.

Nine o'clock at night, and there was a dinner party in full swing. Everyone would be in the dining room and they'd be drinking. The front door would be unlocked, and the security system switched off. He strolled up the drive and walked in. He'd never burgled a house when there was someone at home. Sweat-beaded brow, nerves thrumming though him, he thought he couldn't rely on his knees to carry him. But this was the perfect job, stealing a painting that had already been stolen. Nobody could call the police. Nobody could make an insurance claim. They'd already done that, and, Callum noticed, built a new kitchen with the money.

The Constable was on the wall. He'd known it would be.

He could hear people talking, laughing. A smell of booze and cigars. They'd cooked steaks.

He unhooked the painting. Put it in his game bag, noticed three pound coins on the table below it, and took that too. Expenses. Out the door, down the road and onto a number twelve bus back to Portobello and to Lily.

'Got something for you.'

'Oh, my,' she clutched it to her, 'where did you get it?'
He told her to ask no questions and she'd hear no lies.

Lily died three weeks later. Callum went to the funeral, and afterwards, to the house for ham sandwiches and a glass of sherry. Wandering, glass in hand, he came face to face with Hamish, Max and Lily's son.

'Pity about the paintings,' said Callum.

'Yes,' said Hamish. 'Lily loved her paintings. She took one with her.'

'Where?'

'To wherever she's gone. Heaven, I hope. She got cremated with that damn Constable in the coffin.' He saw Callum's face. 'Doesn't matter. It was a forgery. Family joke.'

So, Callum went home. Walking again; Fran had the car. He stopped at the supermarket to buy some bread. A woman was standing by the magazines at the door. She looked about, then slipped a couple of glossies and a paperback into her bag and walked out. Her face wasn't slippery, just sad; a lonely defeated look. Maybe someone she loved had recently told her she was useless. Callum watched her go and thought, there goes me.

place b.

CHRISTOPHER BROOKMYRE

She stopped at the gate and spent a moment taking in the shiny new sign bolted to the wall outside the terraced premises half way along Pilrig Street. The name was picked out in friendly but calm colours, the typography sparky without seeming frivolous. 'place b。' it said, all informally lower case, the full stop an open, bubbly circle rather than a closed black spot. 'Where you'll find a genuine alternative to medicine,' it explained in a smaller font beneath the logo. Along the bottom, in a more sober typeface, she could read precisely who, and by what credentials, was offering this alternative:

'Char. Litton, Consultant. KU. AK.'

She proceeded to the front door, where she rang the bell and was promptly greeted by a smartly dressed young woman who accompanied her to a small waiting room-cum-office. The young woman sat herself behind a reception desk and took her name, checking the appointment details on her computer.

'Just take a seat, Mrs Cooper, and I'll inform the consultant that you're here.'

She sat on a fresh-smelling leather bench as the receptionist lifted the handset and pushed a button on her phone. 'Mrs Cooper for you, sir,' she said quietly.

She barely had time to lift the copy of *Alt. Health* magazine that was sitting on a low table, before a door opened at the far end of the waiting room and a fair-haired man in his forties emerged with a welcoming smile.

He wore a charcoal suit but no tie; instead opting for a more relaxed light grey V-necked top. Rather than merely hold the door, he came right through into the reception area to bid her his greeting and accompany her personally into the consulting room, where he guided her towards one of two high-backed reclining chairs upholstered in the same soft, dark brown leather as the bench. Along one wall she could see a rather clinical-looking tall cupboard and worktop, bearing a computer monitor, a phone, a thermometer and some glass beakers. However, the rest of the room was in reassuringly marked contrast to the tone and decor she had encountered in any GP's surgery. The room was spacious, high-ceilinged and airy, its spotless, pastel-painted walls adorned with large-framed photographs of brightly coloured landscapes. There were plants and fresh-cut flowers, classical music playing quietly in the background.

She had no sooner taken her ease than the receptionist appeared, to offer a choice of herbal teas. No, quite definitely not like any GP consultation, and she hadn't opened her mouth yet.

'Now, Angela, what can I do for you? Or would you prefer if I call you Mrs Cooper?'

'No, Angela's fine, Doctor.'

'Good, though I have to stress that it's not "doctor". I'm a consultant, though either way, it's Charles, please. I don't find it helps anyone for practitioners to put up these sorts of barriers between themselves and their patients. We have to have real communication between us, a genuine connection, before we can ever truly help each other.'

Angela nodded in earnest agreement, at which he smiled.

'That's why I believe that before you start telling me what's wrong with you, you should instead begin by telling me what's *right* with you. I want you to tell me about yourself, your whole self, because I'm here to treat a person, not a condition, do you understand?'

'Absolutely,' she insisted.

'I mean, you can give a condition a name, but no two people get the cold the same, do they? For some lucky ones it's a sniffle into a few hankies, but for others it's three days in your bed.'

'More like a week,' she said, with a roll of her eyes.

'Tell me about it,' he replied, laughing a little. Then he sat forward in his recliner and said again, more softly, more invitingly: 'Seriously, tell me about it. Tell me *all* about it.'

She talked and he listened, very occasionally making an interjection, usually by way of encouraging her to expand further. She only realised how much time had passed when she went to lift her herbal tea and discovered that the cup and its contents were cold.

It had been close to an hour and she had barely scratched the surface of how she was feeling. Nonetheless, she felt assured that he understood her. She felt there was a connection, and that was the crucial thing. He *listened.*

She'd never had a consultation with her GP like this. Never paid a hundred quid to see her GP either, but she was already feeling like it was money well spent and he hadn't given her anything yet.

'So what do you reckon, doct . . . I mean, Charles. Any hope for me?' she asked, with a little chuckle.

'I reckon we've barely dipped our toes,' he said, further proving that he got what she'd been telling him. 'But I think I can prescribe something to be going on with.'

He got up and walked across to the cupboard, taking several small, thin packets from a cabinet and placing them in a pile on the worktop.

'Are these homeopathic medicines?' she asked, with a slight degree of anxiety, all of it concerned with the possibility that the answer might be in the negative.

'Yes and no,' he said. 'These are not, strictly speaking, homeopathic, but they work on a very similar principle. The pills we prescribe here at the place b₀ clinic have a success rate almost identical to homoeopathic medicines. Better, in some cases.'

'What's the difference?'

'Well, at the risk of blitzing you with too much jargon, our pills have clinically proven effects, as well as what are technically classified as "non-disproven therapeutic benefits".'

'That sounds great,' she said, with an almost impatient sincerity. 'It really, really does. I've tried all sorts of things, but nothing my GP has prescribed has –'

'I understand,' he interrupted, 'but I must insist you take these in tandem with your GP prescription, not instead of. It's a professional courtesy as much as anything else; not that it's always reciprocated. The thing is, we can't go completely abandoning conventional medicine, can we?' he asked with a smile.

She shook her head: the prospect had crossed her mind.

'See, I have a lot of doctor friends still practising conventional medicine, and we in the alt-health world need to keep an open mind about their remedies just as they need to do so about ours. Though I have to say, it's quite annoying when somebody who has been taking alternative remedies for ages gets a prescription from their GP and then, when their condition clears up, gives the GP's pills the credit, simply because that was the most recent thing they took!'

He handed her the packets of pills, plus her dosage instructions, and accompanied her back to the waiting room, where she took a firm hold of his hand as she expressed her thanks, clutching her pills in her other fist.

'Now, just before you go, remember it's vital that you let me know how you are getting on, so come back in a week or so. The more I know, and the more I know about you, I may decide a different place b₀ remedy is more suited to you. Again, it's about you, not about what's *wrong* with you.'

She thanked him again, then turned eagerly to the receptionist, who had her bill prepared and waiting.

A few minutes later, she was back on Pilrig Street, looking once more, this time with some satisfaction, at the sign on the wall:

place b₀

Where you'll find a genuine alternative to medicine

Char. Litton, consultant. KU. AK.

Charles Litton. That's me. Except it's not. My name is Jack Parlabane, and I'm a journalist, working an angle on a multi-million-pound scam. When I tell you the details of what I was up to, it may seem like a lot of work just to get a story, but sometimes the long game is merely a matter of time and patience rather than effort.

Plus, at a hundred sheets an hour from the likes of Mrs Cooper, I was more than covering exes.

Here's the script. I'd admit that in my opinion you can always tell somebody is seriously struggling to make their case against an idea when they say the money could better be spent on schools and hospitals. However, it wouldn't be hypocritical of me to say that it fair boils my piss to know that every year millions of pounds of the money that's supposed to be *for* hospitals is spent on giving people sugar. Let's be clear: I don't mean any kind of metaphorical spoonful of sugar to help the medicine go down, I mean no actual medicine, just very, very expensive sugar.

So who's behind this super-scale fraud? Tate & Lyle? Trust me, if they could command these sorts of prices per gramme for *their* sucrose products, they'd be buying out Microsoft. No, to get individuals, not to mention health authorities, to shell out this kind of coin on sugar (I'm not kidding with this: *sugar, for fuck's sake!*) requires a little bit of hocus-pocus known by the name of homeopathy.

Yep, here's where I'm going to lose a few of you, because you – or at least people you know – utterly swear by the stuff. I'm not saying it isn't popular: that, in fact, is the problem. More than forty per cent of NHS GPs either prescribe it or refer patients to homeopathists; thirty per cent of health authorities fund this kiddy-onny medicine, and a few years back the taxpayer swallowed a twenty million pound refit of the Royal London Homeopathic

Hospital, one of five such institutions funded by the NHS. The Royal Household has enthusiastically employed and endorsed homeopathic remedies for several generations (who said inbreeding lowers intelligence – shame on you), with Prince Charles an extremely high-profile public advocate. And to Buckingham Palace's endorsement, we can add that of the Palace of Westminster too, where in 2007, 206 MPs signed an early day motion in support of NHS homeopathic hospitals.

'The onus is less on homeopathy to prove itself than on its detractors to prove it necessarily does not work,' said one of them, that cheeky chappy Lembit Opik, demonstrating that it's not only his name that's silly. Try substituting the words 'voodoo' or 'sorcery' or 'goat-sacrifice' for homeopathy in that sentence, then see if it's easier to spot the minor philosophical flaw in the principle.

But, for Lembit's benefit, here's a very good indication that homeopathy doesn't work: if it did, then every pharmaceutical company on the planet would be marketing the stuff for all they're worth.

The remarkable but little-understood human ability to self-heal is often triggered by the mere belief that a given remedy will work, or even simply by the belief that one is in good, caring, *healing* hands. Hence this effect can often kick in when a patient has had a one- or two-hour consultation with a solicitous 'alternative medicine' practitioner in a calm and cosy environment, as opposed to an NHS-average seven-to-ten-minute consultation with a harassed GP in a coldly clinical and often dilapidated surgery.

Homeopathy advocates like to make out that they're in the vanguard of exploring this self-healing phenomenon. Problem is, they want to have their cake and eat it. You can't claim to be peddling a therapeutic pill *and* claim to be triggering a psychosomatic response. It's a medicine or it's a placebo: it can't be both. And until they admit their sugar pills *are* merely placebos, homeopathy is not in the vanguard: it's just in the way.

Take Dr Timothy Cullis, head of the Royal Edinburgh Homeopathic Hospital. (It doesn't have a casualty department, in case you ever have an accident and it happens to be the nearest facility: sugar can be sticky, but it's not so effective taken orally when you're trying to glue someone's limbs back together.) According to Timmy, when asked by a Holyrood committee about the remarkable similarity between the results his remedies recorded and the results achieved by placebos: 'It seems more important to define if homeopathists can genuinely control patients' symptoms and less relevant to have concerns about whether this is due to a "genuine" effect or to influencing the placebo response.'

(Now, I'm not a doctor, but I'd have thought it was more important to concentrate on that whole 'genuine effect' thing, especially if we're shelling out millions of pounds each year for a few hundred quid's worth of sugar.)

Timothy's point was that the whole homeopathic doctor–patient loveliness was an inextricable part of a holistic process, hence not only can't you isolate the 'medicine' itself for testing, nor can you ask homeopathic practitioners to participate in double-blind placebo testing. The homeopathist even knowing it's a randomised possibility that he's prescribing a placebo could, apparently, somehow interfere with the magic. Something of an impasse in research terms, I'm sure you'd agree.

So how come I was calling myself Charles Litton and seeing patients at the shiny new place b₀ alternative medicine clinic? Well, some time back I happened upon an extremely valuable piece of information, and consequently devised a means of constructing a genuinely double-blind experiment: one in which not only neither the patient nor the homeopath knows whether placebos are being prescribed, but in which neither even knows they are part of the test.

In clinical terms, it's what's known as a crossover trial, though in this instance double-crossover might be nearer the mark.

The key to it all was a small company called Vitacron. I read about them briefly in the local evening paper, in a piece about the regeneration of a rather run-down light-industrial estate in Corstorphine. I wasn't even reading the piece, just skimming through the story next to it, about an archaeological find in Liberton, when my eye happened to catch the phrase 'exclusive contract to supply several key drugs to the Royal Edinburgh Homeopathic Hospital'. Vitacron, it turned out, were the REHH's conveniently local sole source of Bryonia, Chamomilla, Arsen, Nux Vom and Alconite, five of its most commonly prescribed remedies.

If the REHH practised alternative medicine, then it would be fair to say that I was known to practise what might be termed 'alternative journalism', and this little nugget provided the impetus for a wee bit of just that.

Before doing anything, though, I ran the idea past my wife, Sarah. Being a doctor, she was able to provide me with valuable contacts and technical assistance, as well as giving the project an ethical MoT, which it passed, just. However, being my wife, she couldn't allow herself to be *nothing but* helpful, and found it imperative to throw down a familiar condition.

'You are not allowed to go breaking into this place, Jack,' she told me, and not in a smiley, jokey, but-I-know-you-will-anyway-you-incorrigible-sexy-thing-you kind of way.

Busted – but not all the way back to the drawing board. Rather, Sarah's insistence led to a fairly inspired refinement of the scheme, so I was able to give her my solemn promise. Besides, she only said *I* wasn't allowed to go breaking into the place.

It took only a few weeks to get place b∘ up and running, with the choice of decor and furniture the most taxing aspect of the start-up process. Fortunately, you don't need any kind of licence or indeed any authorised credentials whatsoever in order to set yourself up as an alternative therapist. As of May 2008, you're no longer allowed to make specific claims about your practice without proof of therapeutic effectiveness, but nobody in this business was dumb enough to do that. Keep it vague, that's the key. Never tell them what you're trying to achieve and the punters can never claim you didn't deliver. Look at Boots, for instance. On every high street, they're flogging packets of homeopathic pills bearing the keys-up, cannae-catch-us phrase: 'without approved therapeutic indications'. Seriously. It tells you on the fucking box that the pills don't do anything, but it's proven no impediment to sales. That's Boots as in 'Boots the Chemist', though perhaps it ought now to read 'Boots the snake-oil peddlers'.

I took out some ads in local papers and a few carefully selected publications, while Sarah got some GP friends of hers to make some referrals. The patients they recommended me to were not misled about anything other than my name. They were informed that this was an experimental therapy, that I was not medically qualified, that the remedies I was likely to prescribe were not clinically proven, and that nor would any of it come cheap. All of these warnings proved as effective a disincentive as the admission on the Boots packets. The plan was that I would front this charade one day a week. In practice, I found myself opening three and could have filled the diary for five. The thought that I was in the wrong business did cross my mind a few times as I overheard my friend Laura, who was posing as my receptionist, speaking on the telephone politely turning new patients away.

Sarah's connections allowed me to furnish myself with a generous supply – a superabundance, in fact, despite my clinic's popularity – of official, clinical test-standard placebo pills. However, cheap as these came, it pays to shop around, so I also set up an account with Vitacron and placed orders for several of their signature products. Being an enthusiastic, new and locally based customer, I felt I ought to introduce myself personally to my new supplier, and suggested the ideal time to do so might be on a guided tour of their facility. Vitacron's sales manager Sandy Gifford heartily concurred.

The operation was accommodated within a compact little two-storey compound, a brand new construction largely surrounded by Seventies-built low-rises in varying states of disrepair or demolition. On the rainy Tuesday morning when I visited, Sandy was showing the ropes to a shy but eager young trainee lab technician named Carol. I was accompanied by Laura's boyfriend Michael, posing as a student doing work experience at the clinic. He was dressed in a suit and tie for the occasion, but this only served to make him look even more like a student because of the sheer incongruity the effect conveyed. Michael was doing a PhD in astronomy, and his normal dress sense reflected the fact that he and his peers spent a lot of time hanging about in the dark.

Sandy convened us initially in his office, where I asked him to walk me through the company's ordering and shipping procedures. He showed me the place b. orders on his computer screen and explained the serial system that let them track precisely which pills went to which client, down to the individual packet, which bore the corresponding number.

'It's industry standard for British National Formulary pharmaceuticals. Homeopathic remedies aren't required to comply with those regulations, but some of us believe it's only a matter of time before they're either accepted on to the BNF or just forced to toe the same line by new legislation. Either way, we prefer to be ahead of the game.'

Sandy then took us into the lab, where he talked us through the whole process, 'with apologies to Mr Litton, who is bound to be a lot more familiar with this information than young Carol here.'

'Don't take anything as read on my account,' I assured him. 'One can always learn something new. Besides, the theory behind homeopathy is something I never tire of hearing,' I added truthfully, though neglected to elaborate that this was because it gets funnier every time.

'The father of homeopathy was a German physician by the name of Samuel Hahnemann,' Sandy began. 'The term comes from the Greek: *homos* meaning similar and *pathos* meaning suffering, giving the principle that like cures like. This principle wasn't Hahnemann's, though: it was first suggested in ancient Greek times by Hippocrates, and given that he was the founder of the world's first hospital, we can safely say that he knew what he was about.'

Sandy directed his words mainly at Carol as he warmed to his theme with the alacrity of a proud father telling his kids about the family business.

'Now, back in the 1790s, a trusted remedy for malaria was chinchona bark, which is a source of quinine. Hahnemann was intrigued by the fact that this bark, when taken by a healthy person, caused symptoms similar to malaria, and experimented by taking small doses of it himself, precipitating fever, thirst and palpitations: all associated with malaria. From this, he devised his Law of Similars, as he called it, whereby diseases can be cured by substances that precipitate the same symptoms.'

'Such vision,' I said, smiling and shaking my head with apparent awe, 'to devise such a wide-reaching law on the basis of that single observation.'

Yeah, sarky me, but I had to say something to cover the fact that I was trying very hard to suppress a laugh.

Hahnemann took a tiny quantity of chinchona bark – his reports state four grammes, making the active ingredient utterly minute – and had a very nasty reaction to it, but it never struck the boy that he may simply have been allergic to quinine. Thus was overlooked a simple, rational explanation for the symptoms he experienced, and instead we now have an international pseudo-scientific movement whose founding principle is in fact based on one man's misreading of his own unusual pathology.

'Hahnemann was way ahead of his time,' Sandy went on. 'He understood that these substances could trigger the body's ability to heal itself. You could say he anticipated modern immunology, though he took a different route. Immunology uses small quantities of the disease itself to stimulate the immune system, but the principle is the same, and he pioneered it. Though it's not strictly true to say it was all on the basis of his work with chinchona bark. Hahnemann further experimented with giving people small doses of other substances known to cause disease-like symptoms: arsenic and strychnine, for instance.'

Carol's eyes bulged at this point. 'He gave them poison?' she asked.

'In small doses – ever decreasing doses, in fact, Carol, and you have actually nudged us towards the most amazing discovery at the root of homeopathy. Hahnemann's patients experienced some understandably unpleasant side effects as a consequence of what they were taking, so he began reducing the dosage by dilution. And the astonishing, utterly counter-intuitive result was that the greater the dilution, the fewer such symptoms the patients suffered. Diluting the medicine made it more, rather than less, effective, and thus he came up with his Law of Infinitesimals.'

Michael and I nodded as soberly as we could, but Carol's expression was one of naked incomprehension, wondering did she hear right, wondering perhaps if her faculties just weren't up to grasping this complicated stuff. No, Carol, pet, you heard right and your expression indicates your faculties are serving you well. Break it down: Hahnemann gave people poison, which made them ill. When they took smaller doses of poison, they felt less ill. Contra-intuitive or what! Eat less poison – feel better. What were the fucking odds? And when that's the level of observation and deduction it started from, it's no surprise that homeopathy later progressed to prescribing the same substances to treat completely conflicting maladies. Constipation and diarrhoea, for instance, are both treatable by Sulphur, as we are told on Boots' homeopathy website.

Sandy directed us to a machine housing a number of transparent cylinders filled with clear fluid.

'Dilution enhanced the therapeutic properties of Hahnemann's remedies, and it therefore holds that the more they are diluted, the more effective they become. You follow?' he asked Carol.

'Eh, yeah, okay,' she stumbled.

'I know, I know,' Sandy assured her with a smile (as well as a knowing look to myself: kids, huh?) 'We all find it hard to get our heads around at first. A lot of things in science are counter-intuitive. But as long as you follow the principle.'

'Less is more,' she suggested.

'Very good. And by extrapolation, a lot less is a lot more. Following Hahnemann's method, we take an extract of a substance, which we call the mother tincture, and we dilute it in ten parts water.' With this, he pressed a button on the machine and we watched a small quantity of fluid siphon from one chamber into another. A second button caused the receiving chamber to suddenly vibrate, the cylinder shaken back and forth about a central vertical axis.

'According to Hahnemann, this succussion process is crucial, because it releases dynamic forces within the solution which are intensified with each further dilution.'

'So it's very much a case of shaken, not stirred,' I offered.

'Very good, Mr Bond,' Sandy acknowledged with an approving chuckle. 'And, of course, we then repeat the process, taking the new solution and diluting an extract from it by the same ratio.'

'With the therapeutic effectiveness increasing by a corresponding degree?' Carol asked.

'Indeed. Which is why when we talk about homeopathic solutions, we describe the degree of dilution as their "potency", and the higher the degree of dilution, the higher the potency.'

'How high does it get?' Michael asked.

'Homeopathic dilutions are by the hundredfold, which is why we denote the degree of dilution by the letter c, giving us a 1c for one part in a hundred.'

'So 2c would be two parts in a hundred, or one in fifty?' Carol asked.

'No, 2c would be the 1c solution diluted by the same degree, giving you one part in ten thousand. So you can imagine how potent the solution must be by the time we reach 30c, and some remedies come in at 100c!'

I could vividly imagine how potent the solution would be at 30c. At 24x – that's diluting by a ratio of a mere one in ten, not one in a hundred, twenty-four times – you reach what is known as the dilution limit, meaning that the chances of there being a single molecule of the original substance in any given sample of the solution are very close to zero. At a 'potency' of 30c – that's a one with sixty zeroes after it, by the way – a helping of tincture the size of a teardrop would need to be dissolved in a quantity of water one hundred million times the size of our galaxy.

'But surely, at that level of dilution . . .' Carol began.

'There can't be any of the tincture remaining?' Sandy anticipated. 'Yes, this is the part that baffles the scientists, so don't be too hard on yourself if you're having trouble grasping it. The problem the scientists have is that they are entrenched in thinking about these things in molecular terms. This phenomenon may force them to reconsider a few of their own certainties, something they are unsurprisingly reluctant to do. Truth is, nobody is quite sure how it works, but it is believed to constitute evidence that water has a kind of memory, that water in fact functions almost like a liquid hard drive, and somehow stores information about what has been dissolved in it through changes in its own structure.'

So, to recap, we've got a solution containing no molecules of the original tincture, but this is explained by a hypothesis – with no supporting evidence whatsoever – postulating that water has a memory. But if water has a memory, then what else might water be remembering? We are seventy per cent water ourselves, after all, and, statistically speaking, every breath you take contains at last one atom previously breathed by – and therefore previously constituting a part of – Albert Einstein. That's a far higher concentration of Einstein in your body than concentration of tincture in a homeopathic remedy. Problem is, in the case of homeopathy advocates, the Einstein molecule is diluted entirely in pure-strain pillock, and the paradoxical dilution-improves-efficacy principle doesn't appear to be making these people any smarter. Like cures like, and less is more. I notice, however, that nobody's selling a homeopathic contraceptive. Surely according to Hahnemann's principles, if somebody had a wank and they diluted the sperm . . . or should they get a wee bit of a baby – maybe the umbilical cord – and dilute that?

Sandy led us out of the lab to the automated production line, where trays of pills were being conveyed on a belt beneath a machine dispensing individual droplets.

'And here, as you can see, are the sucrose pillules, which function as the delivery system.'

Yeah. Like I said: sugar.

'A single droplet is absorbed by each tablet, and allowed to evaporate before we place the pillules in blister packs. This, as you will witness next door, is one hundred per cent automated, as it is vital that the pillules are not touched by human hand; even the patient taking them is advised to pop the pack and drop the pill directly on to their tongue.'

'Why?' asked Michael.

'It's due to the risk of them being contaminated by absorbing any substances they come into contact with on the skin, which could render them useless.'

Michael just about suppressed a smirk. I refrained from asking whether sugar's implied memory was as important as water's. Meanwhile, poor Carol looked like she was about to have a vocational crisis.

As Sandy ushered us towards the door to the packaging centre, I announced with an embarrassed apology that I needed to visit the little homeopathists' room. 'All this talk of water and solutions,' I added.

Michael intercepted Sandy as he offered to show me the way, asking a question about the regulation of the droplet volume. I assured him I knew where I was going, which was true: I was going straight back to Sandy's office to access his computer while Michael kept him talking.

With the PC still connected to the local network under Sandy's log-in, I had full-clearance user privileges. I began where Sandy had left off, with my own account details still up when I shook the PC from its screen-saving slumber. I made a few important alterations to my order, involving a small change to the shipping date and a very large change to the quantities.

Next, I pulled up the security section and accessed the plant's CCTV recordings, copying certain files to my flash drive (and when I say copy, I'm talking more ctrl-x than ctrl-c). Thus in a few brief minutes, I laid the groundwork for – but would, crucially, not need to personally execute – the perfect robbery.

★

A short time after my tour, I paid Timothy Cullis a visit at the REHH. The high windows of his dual-aspect office took in the Meadows, the Castle and Salisbury Crags, and I couldn't help but wonder how much normal sugar you'd have to flog to buy a view like that. Timothy was a nervously earnest individual in his late forties who reminded me uncomfortably of Tony Blair. He oozed a cloying, well-intentioned sincerity as he looked you in the eye, but you got the impression some cold, deeper part of him distrusted you on sight and was counting the seconds until you were removed from his presence.

'I appreciate you seeing me at short notice,' I told him, 'but like I said on the phone, this is a pressing matter that I am sure you would want to be made aware of as soon as possible.'

'Yes indeed. Which is why I'm hoping you can be a little less vague now that you're here, Mr Parlabane.' As he spoke, he eyed the black folder I had in my lap. We both knew this was the skinny, but I wasn't cutting to the chase quite yet.

'Certainly. First, forgive me for asking again, but now you've had time to look into it, are you aware of any negative effects being suffered by patients here recently, or any downturn in the effectiveness of your remedies?'

'I haven't really had time to look into it, but very generally, no, everything is running as normal, as far as I am informed. Why shouldn't it be?'

I took the folder from my lap and placed it on his desk.

'I received this yesterday,' I said. 'And though I'm not

obliged to do so, I felt I ought to let you know about it before we run the story.'

I opened the folder and finally showed him the contents, spreading the pages across the broad expanse of sugar-funded mahogany.

'This was sent to me by an anonymous protest group. These are CCTV stills showing the interior of the Vitacron plant in Corstorphine, taken five weeks ago.'

Timothy stood up and lifted one of the images. It showed two blurred figures inside the packing centre, both dressed in black, ski-masks obscuring their faces.

'These close-ups aren't from CCTV: they are from the intruders' own video footage of the break-in. As you can see, they have recorded themselves removing the blister packs from serial-numbered Vitacron packets and replacing them with blister packs of their own. They were very methodical. They took precise note of the range of serial numbers, which you can see on this page here. As detailed in the accompanying letter, these serial numbers should correspond with your orders last month of Bryonia, Chamomilla and Alconite, three of your most commonly prescribed remedies.'

'What have they replaced them with?' he asked, looking as livid as he was worried. It was my guess that 'poison' would be a preferable answer to the one he was truly dreading.

'Sugar. According to the protesters, patients at the REHH prescribed Bryonia, Chamomilla and Alconite have been taking clinical-test placebos for the past month. The placebos by their nature are harmless, but what worried me, naturally, were the consequences of patients taking placebos in place of vital prescribed drugs. However, as you just said, everything's running as normal and nobody has noticed any change, so clearly it could have been a lot worse.'

Timothy swallowed and took a moment to compose himself. He took a step back and folded his arms.

'Clearly' he said, 'this is something that will require more than cursory examination, Mr Parlabane. It may well be a lot worse. I will have to investigate thoroughly, find out when these replacement drugs were prescribed and to whom, bring in the patients concerned and make sure they haven't suffered any harm.'

'Absolutely. How soon can you let me know your findings?'

'I couldn't say. This may take some time.'

'I'll be in touch,' I assured him.

The break-in story ran the next day. Took a bit longer than that for Timothy to get back to me with his findings, not for want of me calling to ask. Nor was there much emerging from the polis regarding the break-in. They were unable to work out how the intruders gained entry without setting off the alarm system, and were further frustrated by the fact that the CCTV files for the night in question had been erased from Vitacron's system.

What Timothy was able to tell me was that there had been little need for him to get in touch with individual affected patients: they had been streaming in unbidden, swamping the hospital's appointments schedule, uniformly reporting deterioration of their various symptoms. I wondered how many experienced a sudden worsening of their condition *before* they heard about the great pill-switch.

To make matters worse for poor Vitacron, they suddenly found themselves clean out of Bryonia, Chamomilla and Alconite at precisely the same time as the REHH was urgently requesting huge quantities of all three to replace the contaminated supplies they'd been forced to junk. Fortunately, Charles Litton was able to come to their rescue. He called up to inform them that some clerical error at Vitacron's end had led to place b₀ taking delivery of massively surplus quantities of Bryonia, Chamomilla, Arsen, Nux Vom and Alconite.

'Probably a computer glitch,' I suggested to the very grateful Sandy. 'I think a couple of zeroes got added to all of our purchases. Either that or we got a hospital order by mistake. Anyway, if you can arrange an uplift and *please* ensure we're not invoiced for this lot . . .'

'Of course, Mr Litton, of course. We'll have someone round to collect the supplies within the hour.'

'The hour? That's sharp.'

'Serendipitous, Mr Litton. You may not know it, but you're a life-saver.'

'Albeit I'm not allowed to make such claims for my therapies.'

Weeks went past with Timothy still unable – or unprepared – to give me an answer. A month slowly turned into two, and two into three. I was patient. I had closed place b₀ after a month, and had my own results, as recorded by the participating GPs, written up and ready to produce when the time came.

After fully four months, Timothy was finally able to report his findings, though not merely to me. He called a press conference in the REHH's lecture theatre, where he was to make a major announcement regarding a breakthrough in homeopathic research. It was a surprisingly busy affair, with journalists present from a few of the nationals, as well as representing several 'body and spirit' (i.e. woo) publications.

Timothy called the room to order and proceeded to read from a prepared statement.

'A few months ago, as you are all aware, some maliciously intentioned and thoroughly uninformed individuals, in a misguided act of protest, broke into the Vitacron facility in Edinburgh and replaced our supplies of three homeopathic remedies with clinical trial placebos. This was the cause of a great deal of upset and distress to many of our patients, to whom we have made our profuse apologies. However, in their attempt to discredit homeopathy, these so-called protesters have in fact inadvertently managed precisely the opposite, because I can reveal that the results of their unapproved double-blind test have been quite the reverse of what I am sure they were anticipating.'

It almost seems superfluous to state that he was looking directly at me when he said this.

'As the paper my assistant is distributing shows, a significant number of patients suffered a marked deterioration in their symptoms as a result of this sabotage. But just as significantly, they enjoyed an equally marked improvement after the resumption of their correct homeopathic prescriptions.

'These, I must stress, were independent, medically

verified changes in symptoms, not merely anecdotal verbal accounts of patients saying they generally felt better or worse. This therefore constitutes very strong evidence of the efficacy of homeopathic remedies as being far and above placebo levels. I will be publishing a paper presenting a more detailed analysis of the results, but even at this early stage, I feel confident that this may be the breakthrough homeopathic research has long been waiting for.'

Timothy then took questions, mainly from the tame hacks of the woo glossies, who teed up for him with lots of 'can you confirm's and 'would you agree's. I waited with easy patience: I'd waited four months as it was, there was no rush. I guessed Timothy wasn't in a hurry to call me either. I was the ghost at the feast, but both of us knew he'd need to give me the floor at some point, being the person who broke the original story and to whom the protestors had sent their materials. It wasn't merely to remind him of this that I held up another black folder instead of merely raising my hand.

'Mr Parlabane,' he acknowledged, with overstated weariness. 'How can I help you?'

'Well, I'd hold off firing into that research paper if I were you,' I told him, removing a page from the folder as I got to my feet. 'There's been a wee development regarding your protestors. They have released the CCTV files they procured covering the night of the break-in. This is a print-out of a frame from one of those files, with a time-stamp matching one of the original stills they sent me. As you can see, it shows the packing centre at Vitacron, but with nobody in it. Here, however, is a still showing the two protestors posing against a blank background. The two images were then combined using Photoshop to create a fake composite. There *was* no break-in. Your patients experienced – how was it you put it? – "a marked deterioration of their symptoms" while taking precisely what they were prescribed here at the REHH.'

Timothy came over a little pale at this point. I toyed with asking if he could do with some Arsen or Nux Vom.

'All of which is not to say that a pill-switch did not take place,' I continued. 'It most certainly did. As Vitacron will confirm, the large quantities of remedies they supplied you to replace your supposedly contaminated stocks were, due to a computer error, originally delivered a couple of days earlier to the place b₀ alternative therapy practice in Pilrig Street. And it was at place b₀ that the close-up footage of the switch was filmed. Again, Vitacron will confirm the serial numbers involved, and they will demonstrate that your patients experienced – once more in your words – "an equally marked improvement" while taking clinical trial placebos.

'The place b₀ clinic, as the name suggests, was also prescribing placebos during its trial month of operation, though the consultation and prescription was carried out by a completely unqualified individual: me. I have the independent, medically verified results of its therapies here for anyone who wants them, and though the sampling is admittedly small, they do show symptomatic improvement levels consistent with every clinical trial of homeopathy. Any comment, Doctor Cullis?'

The look on Timmy's face was . . . well, let's just say it would be vulgar to attempt to place a value upon it.

★

Of course, the final irony was that all of my efforts turned out to have something of the homeopathic about them: i.e. they did absolutely fuck all. Homeopathy remains as popular – and trusted – as ever, and continues to be available on the NHS.

Sugar, anyone?

Carlo Blue

JOHN BURNSIDE

'What's wrong, Jack? Been stood up?'

I turned around. Andy and Ian were sauntering over from the bar, knowing smiles on their faces, as if they'd caught me out in something. Little did they know, I thought, and I cursed myself for being so stupid, meeting Linda in a place like The Commercial. I should have guessed that somebody from the office would be there. So it was lucky, really, that she hadn't turned up. I didn't know Ian that well, but Andy and I went back a fair way, and he'd met Karen at various parties.

I grinned – mischievously, I hoped. 'That's right,' I said. 'Story of my life.'

Their own grins widened in delight at my supposed misfortune, but I could see from Andy's eyes that he wasn't completely taken in. 'So, where's Karen then?' he said.

I looked away, towards the bar. There had been just a hint of genuine enquiry in his voice, and I remembered how he'd taken me to task, once, when he caught me chatting up a temp called Gwen who worked for about three days in Sales and Marketing. 'At home,' I said. I glanced at the door: no sign of Linda, which suited me fine – not just because I didn't want to have to introduce her to Andy, but because, to tell the truth, it had been getting pretty intense over the last few weeks, and her conversation had occasionally veered off into dangerous territory. *Hard but worth it*, *new start*, *don't you want to be together* territory, or even *I'm not sure I can take this any more, it's either her or me* territory – which certainly wasn't where *I* wanted to be. Things hadn't been right at home for a long time, but I wasn't in the market for an alternative. On the other hand, I hadn't helped matters much by going on about how bad it was with Karen. *That* was bound to add fuel to the fire.

'So,' Andy said. 'You're on your own?'

Christ, Andy. Nobody expects the Spanish Inquisition, I thought. I looked at him. 'For the moment,' I said, with slightly more defiance than I had intended. 'The night's still young, though.'

He laughed. 'Well, you can hang about here looking like the dog ate your Viagra. Or you can come with us. We're going over to that new place.' He turned to Ian. 'What's it called?'

'The Balvenie,' Ian said.

'Nah,' Andy said. 'That's a whisky.'

'Well,' Ian said. 'It's *some*thing like that . . .' He pondered a moment, as if he really did have the slightest clue what the name was. He'd had a little more to drink than Andy, or maybe he just didn't carry it as well. 'The Dalmeny?'

'Whatever,' Andy said. He looked at me. 'You want to tag along? Lads' night out?'

'What's The Dalmeny?' I said.

'New restaurant,' Ian said. 'On Thistle Street.'

'New Scots cuisine,' Andy said, with a slight smirk. 'Ian's been. Says it's great. Even if he can't remember what it's called.'

'What the hell is "new Scots cuisine" when it's at home?' I said.

Andy grinned. 'Oh, you know. Stovies with a fancy sauce. That little miracle your old Mum used to perform with an onion, a potato and a tin of Fray Bentos? Same thing, only they charge you twenty quid for it.'

Ian was offended. 'That's not *all* they do,' he said.

I sneaked one last glance at the door, then I finished my drink and nodded to Andy. 'All right, then,' I said. 'Let's go.'

The Ballantrae was only half full and we managed to get a table for three by the window, overlooking the street. It was nicely presented – no tartan, which is always a good thing – and our waiter was a funny, slightly cheeky lad called Kenny, who handed out the menus and, with a big grin on his face, told us what the specials were in Scots.

New Scots Cuisine had capital letters. It was a statement, a culinary experience that would change forever how we thought about the nation's food. The dishes were named and described *only* in Scots, the way things used to be only in French in supposedly smart restaurants; in-your-face, though with a certain mitigating wit in the language and, it had to be said, the food itself was very good indeed. They *did* serve stovies, but they were very *good* stovies and their crannachan – that cliché of Scottish puddings – was, as the food experts on TV always say, a *revelation*. The wine list – also in Scots, with descriptions like *a douce bouguie o whin wi a nynckling o haar* and *fouthie gusts o thimmles an aik* – had been put together by someone who really knew what they were doing. By the time we got there, I had pretty well put Linda's no-show to the back of my mind, and Ian was turning out to be a bit of a character, even if it was obvious that he was twa pieces wantin o a kettle. The only awkward moments came when he, the one smoker at the table, went outside for a cigarette, leaving me alone with Andy, who still thought he'd got a sniff of something not quite right. He wasn't being a pain about it, but when Ian left the table he would give me this odd, questioning look, as if he thought there was something that I might want to confide.

We saw the lights – the police car first, then an ambulance – about halfway through the main course. We'd heard *some* kind of kerfuffle out there a few minutes before, a huge crash and several shocked voices, but then it *was* a Saturday evening on Thistle Street, and after the first shock had died away, we hadn't paid it any mind. After a while, though, we realised that this, whatever it might be, wasn't just the usual Saturday night skirmish. A crowd had gathered outside the pub opposite and people who had been on their way somewhere else came to a sudden halt and stood, with cans or cigarettes frozen in mid-air, transfixed by whatever was going on a little further down the street. I saw a girl's face crumple as she realised what was happening and, I had to admit, I was curious to know what was going on.

I didn't want to let it spoil the evening, though. The stovies were excellent; not at all like the ones Mum used to make. The *thimmles an aik* wine was a very nice Australian Pinot and I was making a mental note to come here again when Ian, who had fairly wolfed down his main course and was already on a second bottle of Chenin Blanc, hopped out of his chair and headed outside for another cigarette.

'God,' Andy said. 'That guy can't sit still for two minutes.' He looked at me. 'So, have you met the new office manager? Archie what's his name?'

I shook my head and had another sip of wine. 'You?' I said, after a moment.

He made a face. 'Oh, *yes*. He's a *real* bundle of joy.'

'Oh? How's that, then?'

I didn't want to talk about work, but then there wasn't anything else to talk about. Not unless we got back to the subject of Karen – and it had been a long time since I'd had anything to say on that subject – out loud, at least. We'd only been married four years and, already, we were like a rerun of my parents, going about our business in a quiet fog of bewilderment and dismay, wondering why the story we had started out with – laughter, sex, actual conversation – had disappeared into thin air. Maybe I wasn't quite the ladies' man Andy suspected, but I wasn't a saint either and there had already been a couple of frantic, if rather short-lived affairs that I'd mostly enjoyed and didn't feel guilty about at all. At least they hadn't been too heavy – but the thing with Linda was a different story altogether. I'd gone into *that* thinking it would be more of the same – there's a lot to be said for ships passing in the night – but she'd had other ideas from the beginning. I had imagined that she knew the score, but it wasn't long before I realised that what *she* wanted was a collision.

*

Andy had moved on from complaining about Archie by the time Ian returned. He'd obviously been out for more than a quick smoke.

'What happened to you?' Andy said. 'Did you pick the tobacco yourself?'

Ian sat down and looked at us. He was a little pale. 'There's a woman been killed,' he said. 'At least I think she's been killed. Somebody drove a car straight into her.'

Andy shook his head. 'Bloody drunk drivers,' he said. Responsible citizens that we were, we had all left our cars at home.

'No.' Ian sounded almost breathless. 'It wasn't a drink driver. It's a woman –'

Andy grunted in mock appreciation. 'Now there's a true gentleman for you. You know, Ian, women get drunk too.'

Ian tried a smile. 'That's not what I meant,' he said. 'I *saw* her. She was sitting in the police car. She drove into the other woman deliberately –'

'No way.'

'That's what they're saying,' Ian said. 'The first one was getting into her car, just minding her own business, and this other one put her foot down suddenly, and drove straight into her. Full speed. Smashed the side of the car in –' He stopped to gather himself together. He wasn't quite there, still, with the dismay of it all and, though some of it could have been the drink, he'd obviously had a real shock, even though he hadn't actually *seen* a thing.

Andy wasn't convinced. Or he didn't want to be. I suppose, like me, he was wishing that Ian had stayed put, or at least that he would have the decency to stop going on about it, now that he was back. I knew a little about Andy's home life and it struck me that, for him, nights like this were too rare to be spoiled by the random actions of some complete stranger. 'Somebody's been having you on,' he said. 'It will just have been an accident.'

Ian looked confused. Then he turned to me. 'You should have seen her *face*.'

I nodded. If we could just humour him a little, he would probably let it go. 'Which one?' I said.

'In the police car,' he said. 'The one who did it. She's not upset or *anything*. She's just sitting there, cold as ice.' He gave an odd, childish shudder. 'I've never seen a face like that on a woman –'

'All right, Ian,' Andy said. 'That's enough now. We're trying to enjoy ourselves here.'

Ian turned to him, then back to me. 'I'm sorry,' he said. 'I didn't mean –'

'Never *mind*,' Andy said. 'Let's have some more wine. You'll have some more wine, won't you, Jack?'

I didn't really want more wine – the wind had gone out of my sails a bit – but for Ian's sake I nodded. We'd have to make the best of things and spin the meal out a while longer, at least until they cleared up the mess outside. I looked out of the window. The crowd opposite had mostly gone back into the pub, leaving just a few stragglers in the road. Whatever they had seen, it hadn't bothered them as much as it had Ian. For them, it was just another one of those strange events that happened on a Saturday night. For Ian, though, it was something else. I mean, it wasn't so much that he was upset; it was more like he was scared. That woman, that look on her face, had frightened him.

'Ian?' Andy spoke very quietly, gently, the way you might speak to a spooked horse, or a bird that had got into the house and needed to be gathered up and freed.

'Sorry?' Ian looked at him, then at me again. 'I didn't hear . . .'

Andy smiled patiently. 'I said, would you like some more wine?'

Ian considered the question for a moment. By then, I thought wine was the last thing he needed. He'd have been better with a brandy, or a nice cup of tea. 'Yes,' he said, as if the idea had come as a pleasant surprise. 'I'll have some more.' Then he glanced out of the window and his face went dark again. He was like a child, when there's a scary movie on and he's too frightened to look at the screen, but not quite able to look away, either. 'Thanks,' he said. 'Good idea.' A fleeting half-smile passed across his face. 'I mean. Thanks. That would be nice.'

We skipped the puddings after that. The ambulance was soon gone, but it was a while, still, before the police car left – and I wondered why they had kept the woman there so long, sitting in the back of the patrol car, where anybody could see her. I suppose, for Ian's sake, we should have sat a little longer, but we fairly raced through that last bottle of wine and, by then, we'd all had enough. I was wishing I'd stayed at home, Ian was still only half there – but it was Andy who seemed the most upset now. I don't think *that* had anything to do with what had happened out on the street, though. He'd probably been looking forward to this night out for ages – maybe Maggie was away somewhere, and he'd been glad of a chance to get out and about on his own. Have a bit of fun, for once. I'd heard it said in the office that he was well under the thumb these days, and from my two or three encounters with Maggie, I wouldn't have been surprised. He wasn't obviously nasty about it, or anything, but you could see that he was fed up. When we came to settle the bill, he made a big performance out of it – how it was going to be his treat, how he wanted Kenny to put the whole meal on his card. The lad was wise to this little piece of theatre, though. He knew that old, Scottish male, displaced aggression deal. If there's nobody to lash out at, the next best thing is to insist on paying for everything. He'd probably been through that one a hundred times.

Outside, the air was cool and clear. It was fairly quiet now and, other than the stoved-in car and the fragments of glass all over the road, there was nothing to show that this Saturday night had been different from any other. Something always happened on a Saturday night. Somebody got drunk and did something crazy, somebody else got drunk and fell in love, or into marriage, or out of both. Somebody got hurt, maybe killed. We would read about it in the papers, no doubt, and it would turn out to be some stupid misunderstanding – some minor incident that had escalated out of all proportion, or a long-held grudge, or maybe just a case of mistaken identity, and we would wonder at the sheer unpredictably, or pointless anger, or pettiness that human beings can muster up. I looked at Ian.

'How are you *doing*?' I said.

He set his mouth, the way a child does when it is being brave, and I wondered how old he was. Whether he was married. He'd been working in the same offices as me for almost a year now, and I didn't know a thing about him. 'I'm fine,' he said. 'I'm sorry about before. It was just . . .' He shrugged. He didn't know what had happened, but I could see that he felt diminished now, in my eyes, and Andy's, and in his own.

'It's all right,' I said. 'Sometimes things just get to you. No need to apologise.'

I turned to where Andy had been standing for agreement, hoping he'd give the boy some moral support – but he wasn't there. He was ten yards down the road, and he was staring at the wreckage. That seemed odd, because I would have imagined he'd want to get away from that, maybe even try and save his evening somehow. Go on somewhere. Play while the cat was away. Then, as he turned back, an unhappy look on his face, I looked at the car myself, for the first time. It was caved in all along one side, the windscreen and side windows were smashed, and when I looked more closely I could see that the dent in the door was reminiscent of a body, an actual impression, like a child's handprint in a block of Plasticine.

But then, maybe I'm imagining that. Maybe I imagined it then, because I'd heard Ian's story, and maybe I imagined it later, when I saw what I had done. What I wasn't imagining, though, was the make of that car – a 1.8 Corolla, like the one I had at home – and the colour – Carlo Blue – and then, as it dawned on me and my mobile started ringing in my breast pocket, the sequence of letters and digits on the licence plate, which – though I knew it couldn't be – was exactly the same as my own.

Driven

IAN RANKIN

I'm the one you all hate, the one you've been hearing and reading about. I was a hero for a short time, but now I'm the villain. Well, not *the* villain. Do you want to hear my side of the story? I have this need to tell someone what happened and why it happened. Here's the truth of it: I was brought up to believe in the sanctity of life, and this has been my downfall.

I am a son of the manse. A curious phrase; it seems to be used by the media as shorthand of some kind. But it happens also to be true. My father was a Church of Scotland minister in a career spanning nearly forty years. He'd known my mother since primary school. I was their only child. In my late teens, I calculated that impregnation (a word my father would have used) probably took place on their Isle of Mull honeymoon. Early July they were married (by my grandfather, also a kirk minister), and I entered the world on April 1st the following year. A hard birth, according to family legend, which may explain the lack of brothers and sisters. My mother told me once that she feared I'd been stillborn. Even when the doctor slapped my backside, I merely frowned and gave a pout (family legend again).

'I knew right then, you'd grow up quiet,' my mother would say. Well, she was right. I studied hard at school, did as little sport as possible, and preferred the library to the playground. At home, my father's den became my refuge. He'd collected thousands upon thousands of books, and started me with parables and other 'wisdom stories', including the Fables of Aesop. I grew up, quite literally unable to hurt a fly. I would open windows to release them. I would lift worms from the baking summer paths and make a burrow for them with a finger-poke of the nearest soil, covering them over to shield them from the sun. I turned down my parents' offer of pets, aware that everything had to die and that I would miss them terribly when the time came. Nobody ever called me 'odd'; not until very recently. But then you know all about that, don't you?

What you can't know is that I thought my upbringing normal and untroubling, and still do. After school, there was university, and after university a lengthy period of speculation as to what should come next. Lecturing appealed, but I was torn between Comparative Religion and Philosophy. I could train for 'the cloth', but felt two generations of church service was perhaps enough. It wasn't that I didn't believe in God (though I had doubts, as many young people do); it was more a feeling that I would be better suited elsewhere. My father had taken to his bed, in thrall to the cancer which had slumbered inside him for years. My mother was strong, and then not so strong. I helped as best I could – shopping, cleaning and cooking. Between chores, I would retire to the den – it had become mine by default – and continue my studies. I learned at long last to drive, so as to be able to visit the supermarket, loading the car with porage oats, smoked fish and loose-leaf tea, tonic water, washing-powder and soap. Once a week I wrote out the shopping-list. Other days, I stayed home. Sometimes we would manoeuvre my father into the walled garden, a rug tucked around him, the transistor radio close to his ear. My mother would pretend to weed, so he couldn't see she wasn't able.

Then the day came when he asked me to kill him.

The bed had been moved downstairs, into the sitting-room. There was a commode in one corner. Some furniture had been removed from the room, meaning the hallway was more cluttered than before. A few of his old congregation still visited, though my father was loath to let them witness his deterioration.

'Still, some people find it necessary,' he told me. 'It strengthens them to see others weaken.'

'But it's kindness, too, surely,' I answered. He merely smiled. It was a few days after this that, having just accepted another small beaker of the green opiate mixture, he said he was more than ready to die. I was seated on the edge of the bed, and reached out to take his hand. The skin was like rice-paper.

'That stuff you keep giving me – don't think I don't know what it is. Liquid morphine. A couple of glassfuls would probably do the job.'

'You know I can't do that.'

'If you love me, you will.'

'I can't.'

'You want to see me get worse?'

'There's always hope.'

He gave a dry chuckle at that. Then, after a period of silence: 'Best not say anything to mother.' I know now what I should have said to him: it's *your* fault I'm like this. *You* made me this way.

It took him another six weeks to die. Three months after his funeral, my mother followed him. They left me the manse, having bought it from the Church fifteen years before. The parish had moved the new minister and his young family into a new-build bungalow. After a time, I was forgotten about. My parents' old friends and parishioners stopped visiting. I think I made them feel awkward. They looked around the rooms and hallway, as if on the lookout for expected changes of decor or ornament. The bed, freshly made, was still downstairs. The commode was dusted weekly. The lawn grew wild, the beds went unweeded. But curtains were changed and washed seasonally. The kitchen gleamed. I ate sometimes at my father's old desk, a book propped open in front of me.

The years passed.

I became a keener driver – maps plotting my course into the countryside around the city, then further afield: west to Ullapool; north to the Black Isle. One daring long weekend, I travelled by ferry from Rosyth to the continent. I ate mussels and rich chocolate, but preferred home. Books travelled with me. I became adept at finding cheap editions in Edinburgh's various secondhand shops. Every now and then I would see a job advertised in the newspaper, and would send off for the application form. I never got round to returning them. My life was busy enough and fulfilling. I was reading Aristophanes and Pliny, Stendhal and Chekhov. I listened to my parents' records and tapes – Bach, Gesualdo, Vivaldi, Sidney Bechet. In the attic, I discovered a reel-to-reel deck with a box of tapes my father had recorded from the radio – concerts and comedy shows. I preferred the former, but concentrated fiercely on the latter. Laughter could be disconcerting.

Oh, God.

I say 'Oh, God' because it's now time to talk about *him*. No getting around it; pointless to tell you any more about my shopping-trips, tastes in music and books . . . All of it, pointless. My life has been condensed. For all of you, it begins with the moment I met *him*. Everything that I was up to that point you've reduced to words like 'bachelor' and 'loner', and phrases like 'son of the manse'. I hope I've shown these to be reductive. I'm not excusing myself; I feel my actions merit no apology. It was a country road, that's all. Not too far out of town, just beyond the bypass. A winding lane, edged with hedgerows. The sun was low in the sky, but off to one side. Then a bend in the road. Dvorak on Radio Three. A fence, with trees beyond it. Smoke, but not very much of it. A car, concertinaed against one of the largest trunks. Tyre-marks showing where it had torn through the fence.

I pulled to a stop, but only once I was safely past the bend. Flashers on, and then I ran back. A blue car, leaking petrol, its engine exposed. Windscreen intact, but frosted with cracks. Just the one figure inside. A man in the driving-seat. He was conscious and moaning, head rolling. The airbag had worked. I managed to yank open his door. It made an ugly grating sound. He was not wearing the seatbelt.

'Are you all right?'

It was an effort to pull him from the wreck. He kept saying the word 'No' over and over.

'You'll be okay,' I assured him.

As I hauled him to safety, hugging him to me, his face was close to mine. He half-turned his head. I could feel his breath on my cheek. There was warm blood running from a wound in his scalp.

'Don't,' he said. And then: 'I'll do it again.'

I realised almost immediately what he meant. No accident, but an attempt at suicide. Seatbelt unfastened, picking up speed as the bend came into view . . .

'No, you won't,' I told him.

'Just leave me.'

'No.'

'Why not?'

'I believe in the sanctity of life.'

I had laid him on the ground, a bed of leaves beneath. At first I took his spasm for a seizure of some kind, but he was laughing.

Laughing.

'That's a good one,' he was able to say at last, blood bubbling from the corners of his mouth. Another car had stopped. I walked towards it, hoping the driver would own a mobile phone. There was an explosion of hot air from behind me. The crashed car was on fire. The heat was bearable. The injured man, I realised, had craned his neck so he could watch me rather than the explosion. His shoulders were still shaking. A young couple had emerged from their open-topped sports-car. I felt sure they would own phones; indeed, led lives which made them necessary.

'You all right, pal?' the male said. He was wearing an earring. I nodded. His girlfriend was wide-eyed.

'Another minute, he'd've been toast,' she commented. Then, fixing her eyes on me: 'You're a hero.'

A hero?

The description would send me to the den that night, to consult any books I could find. I didn't feel like I'd committed an act of bravery. I didn't feel 'heroic'. Heroes were for wartime, or belonged to the realm of mythology. I wished my father were still alive. We could have discussed the notion and its implications.

A police car had arrived first at the crash-site, followed a few minutes later by the paramedics. The driver was sitting up by this time, arms wrapped around his chest. He was in his thirties, around the same age as me. His hair was thick, dark and wavy, with just a few glints of grey. It had been a couple of days since he'd shaved. 'Swarthy' was the description that came to mind. His eyes had dark rings around them. Tufts of chest-hair welled up from beneath his open-necked shirt. His arms were hairy, too. Even when I wasn't looking at him, I sensed he was keeping a careful eye on me. He had been holding a white handkerchief – my handkerchief – to his scalp-wound.

'He was trying to kill himself,' I told one of the policemen. 'That's a crime, isn't it?'

He nodded. 'And we only prosecute the failures.' I think he meant this light-heartedly, but I spent part of the evening mulling his words over, reading meaning into them.

'Did he say as much?' he asked me. I nodded. But later that night a different policeman came to my door with what he termed 'a few follow-up questions'. I learned that the man whose life I had saved was called Donald Thorpe, and that he was denying being suicidal. It was 'just an accident', caused by his lack of acquaintance with the route and some mulchy leaves on the road-surface.

'But he told me,' I insisted. 'He said he would do it again.'

The officer stared at me. His hands were in his pockets. Previously, he'd seemed interested only in his surroundings, but now he asked me if I lived alone. When I nodded, he asked if the house had been in my family a long time.

'It has,' I agreed.

'It's almost like a museum,' he commented, looking around him again. 'You could open it to the public.'

I decided to ignore this. 'Is Mr Thorpe injured at all?'

'Gashes and bruises, maybe some pelvic damage and a rib that'll cause him gyp.' He turned his attention back to me. 'He was dazed when you reached him; might explain what you heard him say.'

I made no reply.

'Papers'll be after you for a picture.'

'Why?'

'They like the occasional feelgood story. You're a hero, Mr Jamieson.'

'I'm not,' I was quick to correct him. 'I only did what anyone would do.'

'Well, *you* were there. And that's all that matters.'

Less than an hour after he left, the first reporter arrived. I started to let him into the house, but then thought better of it – which is why the word 'recluse' appeared in his third or fourth version of the story.

'Just tell the readers what happened,' he explained. 'In your own words.'

'Who else's would I use?'

He laughed as though I'd made a joke. He was holding a tiny recording device, holding it quite close to my mouth. But he was looking past me at the hall's 'cramped furniture and outdated floral wallpaper' (as he himself put it later). I told him the story anyway, deciding to leave out the suicide bit.

'The other couple who stopped,' he said, 'they saw you drag the victim clear as the car burst into flames . . .'

'That's not quite how it happened.'

But it was how he wrote the story up. It didn't matter that I'd told his recorder differently. I became the CRASH INFERNO HERO. When his photographer arrived on my doorstep, he asked me if I had any burns to my hands or arms, any blood-stained or charred clothing. I had already showered and changed into fresh clothes, so I shook my head. The bloodied handkerchief, discarded when the medics had arrived on the scene, was steeping in the sink.

'Any chance we can get a shot of you at the site?' he then asked. But he had second thoughts. 'Car's probably already been towed . . .' He rubbed at the line of his jaw. 'The hospital,' he decided. 'Bedside, how would that be?'

'I don't think so.'

'Why not?'

How could I tell him? Meeting Thorpe, the first question I would need to ask would be: why did you lie? Why keep the suicide attempt a secret? And then: *will* you do it again? (Of course, I *would* meet Thorpe again, at his hospital bed. But that was for later.)

After further negotiation, the photographer settled for me on my doorstep, then standing beside my car, arms folded.

'Don't you feel a bit of pride?' he asked. 'You're a bloody lifesaver. What about a smile to go with it?'

I lost count of the number of pictures he took – well over twenty. And as he was finishing, another photographer arrived, five minutes ahead of *his* reporter. And so it went for much of the rest of the night. Even the neighbours became curious and emerged from their homes, to be collared and interviewed by the press.

Very quiet . . . private income . . . looked after both parents up to their death . . . no girlfriend . . . goes out in his car sometimes . . .

The Reluctant Hero.

Quick-Thinking Quiet Man.

Brave and Bashful.

Local Hero.

This last they used most often over the next few days. Faces I hadn't seen for a while came calling – members of my father's congregation, the ones who'd visited him during his illness. A neighbour over the back called to me one day and passed a home-baked cake across the fence. There were more requests from the media for bedside photos. Just a quick handshake. I appeared on two radio shows, and there was even talk of a civic reception, some sort of bravery award or medal. And then, just when it seemed to be quietening down, a call from the police.

'He'd like to see you. I said we'd pass on the message.'

Meaning Robert Thorpe; Robert Thorpe wanted to see me.

'But why?'

'To say thanks, I suppose.'

'I don't need him to say thanks.' But then again, maybe I did. Maybe in saving his life I'd convinced him that life itself was worth living. And wouldn't it be heartening to hear him say as much?

So I went.

And I wonder now – was that my fatal mistake?

There were only a couple of photographers this time. They were waiting in the corridor outside Thorpe's ward. They had found a young nurse to stand next to the bed. She was to pretend to be changing a drip. I'd be shaking hands with the man I'd rescued. This was all being explained as we walked into the ward. Thorpe was sitting up. Part of his hair had been shaved, and the black stitches in his scalp looked fierce.

'Are you Mr Jamieson?' he asked, holding out a hand. I could only nod that I was. He gripped my hand and the cameras clicked. 'As I keep telling them, I don't remember too much.'

'But you're all right?'

'So the scan says.'

'Just one more, please, gentlemen,' one photographer was saying.

'How about a smile, Mr Jamieson?' asked the other.

'And if our glamorous assistant could lean a little further in towards the patient . . .' (He meant the nurse, of course.)

Then the other photographer took a call on his phone and handed it to me. 'Newsroom want a word.'

More questions, all about how I felt and what had been said to me. Then it was Thorpe's turn to speak.

'Saved my life, so I'm told . . . eternally grateful to him . . . don't know how I'll repay . . . It's all a bit of a blur . . .'

I realised I was drifting towards the swing-doors, keen

to be leaving. But Thorpe waved for me to stay. When he handed the photographer's phone back, he asked if he and I could be left alone for a minute. One of the photographers was asking the nurse for her name and a contact number as they left. There was a chair next to the bed, so I sat down.

'I'm sorry,' I said, 'I didn't bring you anything.' There was nothing on the bedside-cabinet except a plastic jug of water and a beaker. No cards from family, no flowers or anything. Thorpe just shrugged.

'They're letting me out tomorrow.'

'You'll be glad to get home.'

He gave a low chuckle, reminding me of the crash-scene. His eyes were boring into mine.

'"The sanctity of human life".'

'You remember that much then?'

'I remember everything, Mr Jamieson.'

I was silent for a moment. I wanted some of the water in the jug, but couldn't bring myself to make the request.

'Go on,' he said with a smile. 'You're dying to ask.'

'You were trying to kill yourself.' It was a statement rather than a question.

'Is that what you think?'

'You didn't want to be saved. You said you'd do it again.'

'Do what, Mr Jamieson?'

'Kill yourself.'

'Is that what you told the police?'

I swallowed and licked my lips. I could feel sweat on my forehead. The ward was stifling. Thorpe gave a shrug.

'Doesn't matter anyway.'

'*Are* you going to do it again?'

'I'm not going to kill myself, if that's what's bothering you.'

'So it sunk in then?'

'What?'

'What I said to you about the sanctity of life.'

'Is that what you want?'

I nodded again. Thorpe closed his eyes slowly.

'Go home, Jamieson. Enjoy it while you can.'

'Enjoy what exactly?'

The eyes opened a little. 'Everything,' he whispered. To my ears, it seemed louder than any explosion.

You know what happened next.

Thorpe walked out of the hospital and disappeared. It was a couple of days before neighbours began to complain of a smell in the tenement stairwell. Police broke down the door on the second floor and found two bloodstained corpses. Ten days they'd been there. Both men had been unemployed. They'd shared with a third, and he was missing. His name was Robert Thorpe. The car he'd crashed had belonged to one of the two. There were signs in the living-room that a card game had been underway. Poker, according to reports. Cigarette butts littered the carpet. They had been emptied from one of the murder weapons – a solid glass ashtray. It had been reduced to fragments by the force of impact against the first victim's skull. Three empty bottles of vodka, traces of cannabis, the remains of a dozen cans of super-strength lager . . . The second victim had attempted escape but made it only as far as the hallway. He had been punched, kicked and bludgeoned in what the media kept referring to as a 'sustained and horrific assault', quoting one of the police officers.

Questions were asked. Why had police not checked on the flat in the aftermath of the crash? Why had none of the neighbours come forward earlier? What did it say about the state of our society that no one had intervened?

And why had Richard Jamieson felt it necessary to save the killer's life?

THE MONSTER WHO LIVED – that was the headline I'll always remember. Thorpe was pictured in his hospital bed, shaking my hand. It seemed to me that the pretty nurse should have been in the shot, but she wasn't. I was aware that software existed which could alter photographs. I wished they'd used it on me instead of her, but of course I was the subject of their follow-up stories. The journalists were back at my door. They wanted to know if I felt anger, embarrassment, even shame.

'Aren't you ashamed, Mr Jamieson?'

'Shouldn't he have been left to die?'

'Don't you regret . . . ?'

'Didn't he say anything . . . ?'

I stopped answering the door. I left the house only in the middle of the night, shopping at the 24-hour supermarket on Chesser Avenue. I kept the curtains closed in the den. I ate from tins and drank from cans. I even let the bin go uncollected, so they couldn't accost me as I walked up the path with it to the pavement.

Did I feel angry? No, not really. But I better understood the situation a few days later when he killed again. A shopkeeper this time, the event caught on the security camera which had been installed to deter shoplifters. It had failed to deter Thorpe. His haul consisted of cigarettes, alcohol and cash from the till. The victim left behind a wife and five children. My doorbell rang and rang. The voices called questions through the letter-box. One of them pretended to be a postman with a delivery. I opened the door.

'He's killed again, Mr Jamieson. Do you have anything to say to the grieving widow? She wouldn't be a widow if you'd . . .'

I slammed the door shut, but could still hear his voice.

Your father was a man of the church . . . your grandfather, too . . . how would they feel, Mr Jamieson?

Did I feel regret?

Did I feel shame?

Yes, yes, yes. Most definitely yes. And anger, too, eventually, as the meaning of his words sunk in. He hadn't wanted to be saved because he'd known he would do it again – as in kill again. *Don't . . . I'll do it again . . .* And I had allowed this to happen. I had allowed the monster to live.

The TV and radio kept me up to date with the manhunt. Police questioned me several times. Could I shed any light? I explained it to them as best I could. One of the officers was the same man who'd come to my house that night with the follow-up questions, the one who had doubted Thorpe's attempted suicide. He kept shifting in his chair, as if he could not get comfortable. His face was pale. I knew from the media that the police were under a good deal of pressure. They had let Thorpe go. They hadn't checked his flat. They hadn't noticed that the blood on his clothes belonged to more than one person. They shared a certain culpability with me in the minds of the press.

'If only you'd left him to die,' the officer said as he paused on my doorstep.

'I thought I was doing the right thing.'

'Turns out you were wrong, Mr Jamieson.'

Wrong? But when I rescued him, he was still an innocent man, his crimes a secret. He was victim rather than monster, and I was the hero of the hour, wasn't I?

Wasn't I?

Well, wasn't I?

I turned to my father's library again in search of answers, but found too little comfort. There were books about the nature of evil and the more complex nature of good. Why do we do good deeds? Is it in our nature, or does communality dictate that what is best for others is also likely to be of benefit to us? Do people become bad, or are they born that way? Robert Thorpe's life was picked over in the days that followed. His father had been a domineering drunk, his mother addicted to painkillers. There was no evidence that he had been abused as a child, but he had grown up an outsider. His spells of employment were short and various. Girlfriends came and went. One opened her heart to a doubtless generous tabloid. He watched violent films. He liked loud rock music. He was 'a bit of an anarchist'. Photos were printed, showing the trajectory of the killer's life. A blurry child, clutching a funfair ice-cream. A teenager in sunglasses, no longer smiling for the camera. A man at a party, cigarette drooping from his mouth, sprawled across a sofa with a woman in his arms (her face softwared out, to preserve anonymity).

Lucky her.

*

The manhunt continued, but the media interest began to wane. There were rumours that Thorpe could have disguised himself and headed to Northern Ireland – no need of a passport. From there, it would have been straightforward to cross to Ireland proper. The Western Isles was another possibility. Or far to the south, melting into Manchester, Birmingham or London. His photo was on show at every mainline station, and in shop windows and at bus stops. He had taken around three hundred pounds from the shopkeeper. It was only a matter of time before he struck again.

I started to emerge from my house, as a butterfly from its chrysalis. The neighbours showed little interest. There were no reporters waiting kerbside. But everywhere I went, Thorpe's eyes stared back at me from all those wanted posters. I felt I would never be free of him. I dreamed often of crashed cars, mangled corpses, stained carpets, shattered ashtrays. I reached into my parents' drinks cabinet for bottles of whisky and sherry, but found both foul beyond words. One night, I decided to go for a drive. I hadn't been out of the city since the evening of the crash. I found myself steering the same route, slowing at that curve in the road, headlights picking out the remaining scraps of police tape. From a distance, there was no other sign that anything had happened here. I drove on, stopping at the all-night supermarket on my way back into the city.

Of course he was waiting for me, but I couldn't know that. I parked the car in the driveway. I lifted out the bag of shopping. I unlocked the door of the house. I closed it after me, placing the bunch of keys on the table in the hall, the same way my father and mother would have done. There was a draught, meaning an open window. But I still wasn't thinking as I carried the shopping into the kitchen. Glass crunched underfoot. There was glass in the sink, too, and spread across the worktop. The window-frame was gaping. I put down the shopping and checked the den. Someone had raided the drinks cabinet. I switched on the light in the living-room. He was lying on my father's bed. The whisky bottle was on the floor next to him, emptied. He had his hands behind his head. He had twisted his body to face the doorway.

'Hello again,' he said.

'What do you think you're doing here?'

He had removed the stitches from his scalp. The wound hadn't quite healed. There was a baseball cap resting on his chest. He placed it to one side as he began to swing his legs over the side of the bed.

'I missed you,' he said. 'This where you sleep?'

'I sleep upstairs.'

'That's what I reckoned. Took a look around, hope you don't mind.'

'The window's broken.'

'Windows can be fixed, Richard.'

'How did you find me?'

'Your old man's still listed in the phone-book – Reverend Jamieson.' Thorpe wagged a finger. 'Time you did something about that.'

'You've been killing people.'

'Yes, I have.'

'Why?'

There was that smile again, as if he knew some joke

no one else in the world did. 'I couldn't believe it,' he said, 'when they took me to hospital, cleaned me up and had me checked. And the cops, asking me questions but never quite the *right* questions. Every time those doors swung open, I reckoned I was done for. But they patched me up and then they let me walk right out of there.' He was pointing towards the doorway. He was still sitting on the edge of the bed, and it seemed to me that he was offering me the chance to escape, indicating the direction I should take. But I was too busy listening to his story.

'It struck me then,' he went on, 'that I could do it again.'

'Kill, you mean?'

He nodded, eyes fixed on mine. 'Again and again and again. So tell me, Mr Richard Jamieson, how does that square with your "sanctity of life"? What does the Bible tell you about that, eh?'

When I didn't say anything, he raised himself from the bed and walked towards me.

'Is this where your old man died?' he asked.

I nodded.

He was very close to me now. He had forgotten his baseball cap. He squeezed past me without making eye contact. I followed him into the hall. He turned left into the den.

'This where he spent all his time?'

I nodded again, but he had his back to me, so I cleared my throat. 'Yes,' I said.

'And now it's all yours. We're not so different, you and me, Richard.'

'So biology would have us believe.'

'The old human DNA . . . go back far enough, we'd even be related, am I right?'

'I suppose so.'

'Darwin says the apes, the Bible says Adam and Eve. Do you think Adam and Eve were apes, Richard?'

'I don't know.' He had turned to face me. 'What are you doing here?' I asked him again. 'The police are looking for you.'

'But they're not very clever – we both know that.'

'How clever do they need to be?'

He answered with a twitch of the mouth. 'I've been thinking about you, Richard. Papers have been giving you a hard time. They reckon you should have let me top myself. How do you feel about that?' He was resting the base of his spine against my father's desk, one foot crossed over the other, arms folded. When I didn't answer, he repeated the question.

'Why do you need to know?' I asked him instead.

'Does there always have to be a reason? I'd have thought you'd have learned that much, despite all these bloody books.' He nodded towards the shelves. 'I'll tell you why I wanted to see you again – to thank you properly.' He gave a bow from the waist, still with arms folded. Then he eased himself upright. 'Now, if you'll excuse me . . .'

'What are you going to do?'

'You know what I'm going to do, Richard.'

'You're going to kill again?'

'And again and again and again.' His voice was almost musical. 'And all thanks to you and your sanctity of life. Learned from your father, I'm guessing, years before you watched him wither and die. Were there any words of comfort, Richard? Did he meet his maker with a happy and a fulsome heart? Or had he twigged by then that it's all a joke?' He waved his arm towards the books. 'All of it.'

He waited for my answer, then gave up, brushing past me again as he stepped into the hall.

'I can't let you go,' I told him.

'Good for you.'

'You know I can't.'

I had lifted the bottle of sherry from the cabinet. There was less than an inch of liquid left inside. I was holding it by the neck. He stood there in the hall, waiting with his back to me, head angled a little as if consulting some hidden force beyond the ceiling.

'I know you can't,' was all he said. It was as if he'd become the passenger and I the driver.

I lay down on my father's bed that night, a baseball-cap resting on my chest. Was I hero or villain? I'm hoping you'll tell me. I'm hoping one of you will tell me. I need to know. I really need to be told.

Again and again and again.

Recompense

JAMES ROBERTSON

Thursday 28th October 1852

Am just now returned from the Club, and hasten to scribble this entry, but can hardly hold the pen to write – and this has nothing to do with the very fine bottle of port Charlie Cairncross and I dispatched after dinner! What distracts me is the news – the horrible, fascinating news – which I learned from Cairncross and which was on the lips of every other member present, that my old lecturer in anatomy, Dr Lewis Symington, has been murdered! This is scarcely believable, yet there is no question but that it is true.

According to Cairncross he was found collapsed in the High Street at about one o'clock yesterday morning, having apparently staggered there after being most grievously assaulted. A police constable coming upon Dr Symington at once called for assistance, and he was conveyed to the Infirmary – the very place where he practised, adjacent to the Medical School wherein he gave his lectures – but despite all efforts to save him, he did not regain consciousness, and departed this life at around three o'clock.

Cairncross's connections with the city constabulary seem to give him access to the gruesome details of almost any act of criminality. As an advocate he is obliged on occasion to plead on behalf of some of the most disreputable blackguards in all of Scotland at the Justiciary Court, but whereas most of his fellows regard this as an unpleasant duty, Cairncross seems to delight in it. Be that as it may, he was able to tell me that the trail of blood led back from the place where Dr Symington lay, near the head of Blackfriars Wynd, through a close and a court to a narrow stair that descends towards the Cowgate. It seems that it was on this stair – one of the dingiest and darkest spots, so Cairncross avers, in a veritable warren of over-crowded, dirty, crumbling tenements – that the attack must have occurred. It was a foul night of wind and rain, which is perhaps why nobody has been found who saw or heard anything. No weapon has yet been discovered nor anyone apprehended.

Here is a conundrum: Dr Symington's home is in Heriot Row – I have been there on two occasions myself – so what was he doing in so insalubrious a quarter at such an hour? Often he extended his medical advice and expertise, without recompense, to those of the poorer classes who were otherwise unable to afford them. One may surmise, therefore, that he was on some such errand of mercy when attacked, although the middle of the night seems an odd time for such a venture, and it would surely be more usual for the poor to come to Infirmary Street than for him to go to them. No doubt all will become clearer in time, but what a grisly end to such a distinguished career, and what an indication of the viciousness of the times in which we live! I can only imagine the grief which now hangs over that fine house in Heriot Row. I should send my condolences to Mrs Symington and her daughters – but what can one say in such circumstances that will not add to their already too heavy burden of distress? In any case, they would probably struggle to remember who I am.

2 a.m.
I lay down to sleep, but my mind was too active, and here I am again at my journal. Every time I closed my eyes I thought of that cheerful drawing-room, lit with glittering chandeliers and decorated in the most tasteful fashion, populated by the very finest men and women in Edinburgh society, and the two Miss Symingtons performing a duet at the pianoforte while their father looked on – I was going to say with love and admiration, but he never seemed very affectionate toward them. They are, it is true, neither the most accomplished nor the most attractive of their sex, one having a jaw like the prow of a ship and the other a nose scarcely less prominent. Perhaps Dr Symington despaired of marrying them off. I did at one time consider the possible advantages of engaging the affections of one or the other, but my heart could not be persuaded to make the necessary sacrifice. However, I digress. I thought of that bright drawing-room, and then I thought of the dismal, miserable location where he met his end. What a contrast! I feel I must seek out the spot, and will ask Cairncross to take me there tomorrow. For now, since I can neither sleep nor write any more, I will try to read. The latest issue of the *Edinburgh Medical and Surgical Journal* is at hand and, I am sure, will soon have me nodding.

Friday 29th October
The Scotsman carries a piece this morning, describing the efforts of the police to find a culprit. It is a long article, but contains little information beyond what Cairncross already related to me. There is also an eulogium in which Dr Symington's erudition, surgical skills, charity, moral

character etc. etc. are fulsomely described. It may be some small comfort to his family that he is thus so publicly honoured but I, as one of his least attentive and industrious students, cannot quite see him in so glowing a light. Is it callous of me to write that down? Probably. Do I feel remorse? Not much.

I had two visits to make this morning, both to lady hypochondriacs who are never so sick that they cannot flirt with me, and whose vague and inconsequential ailments I treat with resolute seriousness (that is, I take great care not to laugh), cautious diagnoses, harmless drugs and lengthy bills. I like this trade, since it requires so little effort to be authoritative, and since there exist so many healthy, wealthy people whose principal pleasure in life is to spend their money sustaining a fiction about how ill they are. But today these petty pretences and inventions – on their part and on mine – are somewhat wearisome.

The ladies, of course, were anxious to talk about 'poor Dr Symington' as if he had been their dearest acquaintance, whereas I suspect he acknowledged their existence with little more than a nod or a bow on public occasions. I dispensed half an hour of gossip to each, and will charge them accordingly.

Next I went to Lady Balcathro, who is genuinely incapacitated by old age. At ninety-six she has more years than the other pair between them, yet her mind is twice as agile. She is of such a vintage as to make her that rare thing, a Scotch aristocrat who still speaks Scotch. I arrived and told her what I knew of the affair, but her lively imagination had already worked out to her own satisfaction the motivation for the killing.

'He studied under Liston and Knox,' she said. 'However graund a man Robert Liston micht *noo* be, it's weel kent that in his youth he wad steal yer corp afore ye were cauld in order tae cut ye up and display yer puddens tae the students. As for Knox, weel, ye ken whaur *his* supply o subjects cam frae. I dinna doot but that Dr Symington was up tae the same ploys when he was a laddie, and gaed aboot howkin puir folk oot o kirkyairds or peyin somebody else tae dae it. And noo, I jalouse, ane o his victims' bairns has catchit him on a mirk nicht whaur he shouldna hae been, and Burked him oot o vengeance.'

'My dear lady,' I said, 'you cannot be serious.' But she was – deadly serious. I said that she did not seem to have much sympathy for the good doctor, to which she replied, 'Deed na, and no muckle respect for him either. I never likit him when he was alive, and I canna say I feel ony different noo he's deid. There was aye something sleekit aboot him.' When I pressed her she would elaborate no further, but her opinion, though often enlivened by flights of fancy, is not one I would too readily dismiss.

This evening – another dismal night – Cairncross and I walked down to the Cowgate and entered, at his suggestion, one of the howffs we used to frequent twenty years ago as students. I have not been in the place since, but it has changed little. It has a low ceiling and is frequented by low women, students and Irishmen. It was rather thrilling to drink a glass or two of ale there after such a long absence, and then, slightly intoxicated, to set off along the ill-lit street to find the stair where Symington met his end.

The ease with which Cairncross moves in such

surroundings impresses me. His appearance is quite rodent-like with his red-rimmed eyes, sharp yellow teeth and thick smooth hair, and he seemed completely at home scuttering through these narrow streets and vennels. For myself, interesting though it was to remake my acquaintance with this part of town, I have no desire to make a habit of it.

During our hour in the Cowgate howff we were engaged in conversation by two women whose profession was not in doubt, while a massive rogue with a patch over one eye and a ferocious glare in the other rested himself at another table and watched the proceedings. Beside this mountainous devil sat a young girl of, I would say, no more than fifteen years of age, whose pale, sad, beautiful features made a remarkable contrast with his. Had she not seemed perfectly at ease in his company I would have suspected him of exercising some malevolent power over her. She said not a word but sat patiently all the while, except when she rose on one occasion to fetch him another drink. I may not be the best physician in Scotland, but even to my sometimes less than acute professional eye it was evident, observing her in profile, that she was with child, and very close to the term of her delivery. What was extraordinary, however, was that she looked as innocent of the act of procreation as those depictions of the Virgin Mary one sees in old Italian paintings.

Cairncross was relaxed and indeed seemed to enjoy the badinage that passed between himself and the two women. When at one point he went to speak with the one-eyed man, I felt myself much at a disadvantage without him there to ward off the unforgiving blows of their wit, which they delivered amid gales of hilarity. The Miss Symingtons are less intimidating because more refined. However, they are also less interesting to look at.

I noted that in his exchange with Cyclops it was Cairncross who appeared the master – in spite of his diminutive size – and the other who was acquiescent, although his seeing eye never quite lost its fire, and seemed too often for my liking directed towards me. Cairncross finally returned and said we must be on our way, having purchased them drink – whisky for the women and ale for Cyclops (the girl would take nothing). We duly made our excuses and sallied forth into the night.

I was glad to escape, as to have engaged in much more intimate intercourse with the women would no doubt have endangered our health, while to have taken up more of their time and then spurned them would, I thought, have roused the wrath of their *guardian* and thus led to injury of a different nature. But Cairncross assured me that we were not in any great peril, since 'Khyber Davie', as he called him, was 'a gentle cratur' who would not hurt anyone who did not first hurt his family or his friends.

'How do you come to know this man?' I asked. 'And who was the young beauty beside him?'

'Oh, Davie is a valuable assistant,' he said. 'He acted as a witness for a client of mine some years ago, and since then has helped me by gathering information in other causes – information which it would have been near impossible for me to acquire directly. As to the lassie, she is his niece.'

'She will soon be a mother,' I said.

'Yes,' he said, 'and it is partly for that reason that I took you there tonight. I needed to show you to Khyber Davie, so that if he saw you again he would not be alarmed.'

'*He* alarmed at *me*?' I said. 'What on earth do you mean?'

'I can say no more at present,' he said. 'But should I call upon your assistance suddenly in the next week or two, I trust you will not let me down. It may be in your power to perform a great act of humanity, but if I tell you more now I fear that I would compromise you, and that you, unwittingly and for misguided reasons, might perform a great act of *in*humanity.'

'Charlie,' I said, 'you speak in riddles.'

'Trust me,' he said. 'In time, I promise, I will explain all.'

He then led me to the spot where Symington fell. In the gloom it was impossible to see if any bloodstains remained, but it is unlikely, on account of the heavy rain that fell on the night of his death, and the cold drizzle that has continued since. We followed the route he must have taken to reach the High Street, and paused for a moment at Blackfriars Wynd. Dirty water dribbled down our necks from a broken gutter, and I imagined myself in Symington's place, bleeding profusely, calling for help or perhaps unable to do so, seeing the street spin before me and falling face forward onto the wet, greasy cobbles.

Cairncross said that Symington was stabbed several times in the back and chest. The surgeon who inspected the wounds – a young man called Anderson, with whom I am not acquainted – told him that any one of them would have been fatal. Anderson thought it something of a miracle that Symington managed to get as far as he did, but then he was a powerfully built man, and still fit, although approaching his sixtieth year. Cairncross opined that he was powerful in other ways too, and that he had no shortage of enemies in academic, medical and municipal circles. Yes, I said, but did anyone hold such a grudge against him as to wish to kill him? Surely he was the victim of a random assault, a robbery perhaps?

Perhaps, Cairncross said, but his friends in the constabulary told him that nothing had been stolen. A wallet containing a few banknotes, a gold watch and a silver match-case were all found upon the body.

Then, I said, he must have defended himself so well that his assailant took flight, and it was only after this that he staggered to the street and collapsed.

'Perhaps,' Cairncross said again, and I noticed that he hesitated slightly. Then he said, 'There is, however, one item missing – his bag of medical instruments. It has not been discovered at the Infirmary, nor at the Medical School, nor at Heriot Row. Whether he had it with him or not no one knows, but it has quite disappeared.'

I told Cairncross about Lady Balcathro's theory. He smiled and said he thought it unlikely. 'If I wished to be avenged on somebody for something they had done to me or mine,' he said, 'I would not care to wait thirty years.'

Saturday 30th October

I have had a terrible night. I was beset with nightmares, which I cannot ascribe to the effects of the ale and the two bottles of claret Cairncross and I consumed at the Club after our evening excursion. In truth, I think it was the excursion itself that brought on these horrors. Several times I awoke, drenched in sweat, and at precisely the same moment in the course of a dream, which I now set down: I was making my way along a dark close, and I wanted to turn back but could not because behind me blocking the way was the brute with the eye-patch, Khyber Davie. So I went on and came to a court and crossed it in the rain, and proceeded down a stair. And at a turn on the stair I saw an open leather bag, full of gleaming instruments, and then I saw a woman's body stretched out on the steps. It was one of the women from the howff. Her garments were pulled up to her chest, she was dead and a man crouched over her. He had cut her open, there was blood everywhere, and when he looked over his shoulder at me, it was Symington, with a fiendish grin on his face, and his arms up to the elbows in blood as he pulled her intestines out, and that was the moment I awoke.

I fear I have caught a chill. Mrs Brown called up to ask why I had not come for my breakfast and I replied that I was unwell and did not require any. Having thus offended her housekeeperly sensitivity – for she will undoubtedly blame my lack of appetite on over-indulgence last night – I returned to bed and slept all morning. This afternoon, feeling much better, and the weather being fine at last, I went for a walk through Stockbridge and along the Water of Leith. This evening I dined at the Club. Looked for Cairncross but he was not there.

Sunday 31st October

Slept soundly – no recurrence of the nightmare. Attended kirk at St Giles. Although, being of sound and rational mind, I do not believe anything that issues from the mouths of ministers of religion, yet it is beneficial to keep up appearances. My patients are all church-going folk, and so I must be church-going too. I suspect them all, however, of theological shortcomings: the deeply religious suffer from imbecility, the mildly religious from insincerity, and the intelligent like myself from infidelity. There is more deceit, of one kind or another, gathered in your average Scotch kirk on a Sunday than you would find in all the bazaars of Persia.

Mrs Symington and her daughters were in their pew, all veiled and dressed head to foot in mourning. A kind of space remained around them even though many people stepped forward to utter a few words of sympathy. It was as if they were isolated from the world by the sudden unexpectedness of their grief. The minister mentioned the doctor in his prayers.

Afterwards, I decided to walk to the Palace and through the Park. As I passed Blackfriars Wynd I was tempted to revisit the scene of the murder, when who should emerge like a rat from that shadowy neighbourhood but Charlie Cairncross? He seemed slightly startled at seeing me, or perhaps at having been seen *by* me, but recovered himself and offered to join me on my perambulation. He had been back, he said, to clarify something in his mind. He did not elaborate, so I told him of my dream of the previous night. He had a ready explanation.

'Your mind,' he said, 'in its unconscious state, confused Dr Symington with Dr Knox, and Dr Knox with Khyber Davie. Dr Knox, as you know, is in London now, but did you ever see him when he was still here?'

'Of course,' I said.

'And what was the most striking thing about him?'

'His eye-patch,' I said.

'Quite,' Cairncross said. 'He lost the sight of one eye from smallpox in his youth, and wore a patch over it – presumably still does. Now, several of the victims of his suppliers, Burke and Hare, were prostitutes. Combine these facts, with which you have been long acquainted, with Lady Balcathro's theory, add the information I gave you about Symington's missing medical bag, and the resulting reaction in your brain as you slumbered caused your nightmare.'

We parted company on the London Road and I made my way back to my rooms. After luncheon I picked up the *Medical and Surgical Journal* but soon laid it aside for the latest instalment of Mr Dickens's *Bleak House*, which I found much more instructive. I then passed a solitary evening with another bottle of claret, pondering Cairncross's interpretation of my dream, with which I am inclined to disagree. It is the image of Dr Symington leering at me, and his blood-soaked hands, that makes me think along other lines. I recall rumours from my student days about Symington, but cannot quite think what they were. I do recollect somebody saying that he had been observed in a state of inebriation, entering a house of shame, but there was more, I'm sure. The details, however, are lost to me.

Fitting thoughts, no doubt, for a night when witches, bogles and demons are said to roam the earth.

Tuesday 2nd November

Today was the funeral of Dr Symington. Many came to pay their respects, both at kirk and afterwards at the Grange cemetery. I felt it only proper, despite my bad memories of the man yesterday, to attend the interment. Edinburgh society was there in numbers – doctors, lawyers and other professional men, all, like me, paying their respects whatever their inner feelings towards the deceased. There were no women present, of course. Or rather, there was *but one*, and she uninvited.

I was standing at the back of the mourners encircling the grave, not really listening to the minister's dirge, when I suddenly discerned a solitary figure, fifty or more yards away beneath the trees. To my astonishment I realised it was the young girl from the drinking-den. She was watching the proceedings with the same calmness she had exhibited on the previous occasion. There was, however, something cool, almost chilling, about the way she stood. She seemed utterly impassive, and made no attempt to conceal her advanced state of pregnancy. If she had come any closer, or had been noticed by anybody else, the company would have been scandalised.

As the interment was concluded and the crowd began to disperse, I set off in that direction to see if I could speak with her, but I was obliged to exchange a few words with one or two acquaintances, and by the time I won free she was gone. I am intrigued. She did not come, I am sure, out of mere idle curiosity. There is some connection between her and Symington, and her condition arouses the most outrageous speculation! I have hurried home to write all this down before I go to the Club, where I hope to find Cairncross. It is time, I think, that he shed some light on this delightful mystery.

Thursday 4th November

For two days and nights now I have looked for Charlie Cairncross, at the Club and elsewhere, in vain. He has quite gone to ground. I am frustrated beyond endurance. So too, I imagine, are the police, who are no further forward with finding Dr Symington's murderer. They have been speaking to dozens of the inhabitants of Blackfriars Wynd and thereabouts, but no further information has been forthcoming. Something tells me they should be interviewing Khyber Davie's niece, but to what purpose? It is no business of mine, yet with every day that passes, the chances of an arrest being made must diminish.

Saturday 6th November

I can only conclude that Cairncross is deliberately avoiding me, or has left Edinburgh – but why? It occurs to me that he must know a great deal more about the Symington affair than he has so far revealed, to me at least. But what reason can he have for withholding information from the police?

Saturday 13th November

This last week has been one of interminable visits and consultations – a steady round of aches, pains and imaginary complaints, and one or two unpleasantly real ones. I am heartily sick of being a bad physician, but the truth is I have never applied myself with sufficient rigour to make a good one. Yet of all my patients, only Lady Balcathro is astute enough to understand this. Without her to lighten my day, I fear I would be driven to some desperate measure such as opium or emigration. I have been at her bedside three times this week, reading *Bleak House* to her since her eyesight has become too dim to cope with the print. She said to me yesterday, 'Dinna think I thole ye because I believe ye'll mak me haill again. I hae been ower lang in this warld tae pit faith in fairies or mountebanks. Och, dinna look sae shocked, laddie. We baith ken whit ye are. But I like yer company and I think *that* does me mair guid than ony o yer potions.' I felt as if she had dashed a pail of cold water in my face. It was rather refreshing.

Still not a word from, or of, Charlie Cairncross.

Sunday 14th November

At last! I failed to find him, but he has found me! After kirk I went on the same walk as before, down the Royal Mile and through the Park, and halfway down the Canongate there he was, leaning against a wall, waiting for me. 'Where have you been?' I demanded. 'I will tell you,' he replied. 'In fact, I will tell you all. It is now safe to do so.' And so we walked, and he talked, and eventually we retired to my rooms where he completed his remarkable story. I now record our conversation as nearly as I can recollect it.

'Dr Symington,' he said, 'was not quite the pillar of society that everybody thought. I correct myself – not *every*body, for I have always considered a show of outer respectability to be a sure sign of inner lassitude and vice. I suppose most people – looking, for example, at you and me – would consider us sound, decent men, yet I gamble, we both drink too much and – for different reasons – we have eschewed that condition which is thought an essential sign of moral decency even though we are nearer forty than thirty. Don't look so startled – I mean marriage, not celibacy! Why are you not married? For me, it would be one hypocrisy too many. You seemed none too keen on our lady friends of the other night, yet you are perfectly aware that even in Edinburgh there are cleaner, bonnier versions that do not come with half the expense, let alone all the relatives, of a wife. I daresay you may even have availed yourself of their comforts. As for me, well, we need not go into that. You know what I am and I don't think you care too much.' (As a matter of fact, I have never been quite sure what Cairncross 'is'. He guards his predilections too well.) 'The point I am trying to make,' he continued, 'is that we all have our vices, and it is ridiculous to pretend that we don't. Most vices harm no one very much. But some do, because they are practised by the powerful upon the vulnerable and helpless. Tell me, what did you really think of Symington when you attended his lectures all those years ago?'

'I thought him – at first – strong, intelligent, considerate. He always spoke and acted with firmness and authority.'

'And later?'

'I found him bullying, arrogant and intolerant,' I said, and was quite shocked at the vehemence with which I spoke.

'The coin spun, in other words, and the reverse was revealed. He was not, then, as he at first appeared?'

'I suppose not.'

'Yet you still fluttered at the edges of the social circle over which he presided. You even managed to get yourself invited to his house, and partook of his hospitality.

Why? Because you were like a moth drawn to the bright candles of respectability. Without respectability, you would be unable to conduct your professional life in the way that you do. Am I correct?'

'I don't think I like you much, Charlie,' I said.

'That is because I am pricking your conscience. But I like you, which is why I'm telling you this. And now pay careful attention, while I tell you about Khyber Davie and his niece Mary.

'Khyber Davie was a soldier in one of Her Majesty's many regiments. Not having any rebellions to put down at home, this regiment was sent to India, where there were plenty of ill-natured natives in need of having their ears boxed. Davie was no better or worse than his comrades, but he had the misfortune, about six years ago, to lose an eye in a skirmish with some mountain tribesmen, and, since it was the eye he aimed his rifle with, he was deemed surplus to military requirements and invalided home. He returned to Edinburgh and lodged with his sister and her nine-year-old daughter in a house not far from Blackfriars Wynd. The sister had been a washerwoman, but she had become sickly and wasted after her husband, a labourer, was killed when the half-built wall of a house fell on him. Khyber Davie took up the same kind of work, on the building-sites of Newington, and brought in enough money to keep them from starving. By day he heaved sandstone blocks about, dug drains and carted off rubble, and by night he slept, drank or assisted his niece in the care of his sister, who was hardly able to keep house, let alone work.

'Davie was, as I told you before, a witness in a cause

of mine a while back, and I saw then that he was the kind of man who could be very useful to an inquiring legal mind like mine, and so indeed he has proved. We are not – could not be – friends, but we have grown to trust each other over the last year or two.

'I should say that in the same building they inhabited were two harlots – the very pair you met – who had befriended the girl when she was much younger, and had even looked after her when her mother was too ill to do so. These women were as good as family to Davie, his sister and young Mary, and he often guarded over them while they plied their trade, as you yourself saw.

'So far, you will note, nothing more extraordinary than poverty, bad luck, war, degradation and endless toil had upset the lives of these people. But all that was about to change. On the night of Dr Symington's murder, about two o'clock, I had a visitor. I was still up, working on some papers, when I heard somebody outside my window, calling for admittance. It was Khyber Davie. I let him in at once. He was in a terrible state. He had blood on his shirt and he had a large black medical bag concealed under his coat. He told me that he had just murdered a man, a doctor, that he intended to give himself up directly, and would I represent him if he did so, and secure him a quick sentence? All he wanted was to be put out of his misery as soon as possible. I explained to him that the law did not act in quite that way, and gave him a large whisky. I had no fear of Davie. In fact, I couldn't really believe that he had done what he said he'd done. So I asked him to tell me everything.

'Davie's story was this: last year, his sister's health became even worse than usual. She was suffering severe stomach pains. Perhaps she was dying, perhaps she could be saved. Davie thought that Dr Symington might operate on her, so he went to him and begged him to help. Symington inspected the woman, concluded that she was beyond his skills, and declined to operate. Davie was distraught. But then his niece, Mary, said that she would try to persuade the good doctor. And somehow she did. Not only did Symington change his mind and agree to operate on her mother, but he seemed to take a liking to Mary, who as you saw is a beautiful, naïve-looking child, and offered her a position in his household in Heriot Row, where she could be trained as a housemaid. Davie's distraction was turned to hope and joy. He saw this as a great opportunity for his niece to escape the squalor of their existence. But as he told me this, my heart sank. I knew things about Symington, things almost impossible to prove but which circulated nevertheless, of which Davie had clearly been entirely ignorant when this offer was made.

'Dr Symington was well known for his charity to the deserving poor. I regret to say that few of them deserved *him*. He would generously perform surgical operations for nothing, but he was interested only in difficult cases, where there was a high risk of failure, so wretches with minor, easily corrected ailments need not apply to him for relief. The excision of cancerous growths, intrusions into the deepest recesses of a living body – these were the sort of challenges that excited Symington. And why not? He was a good surgeon, and how else are surgeons to improve their skills if not by trial and error? The deserving poor had little choice: it was go under the knife or die. But there were two difficulties. First, the choice was not really theirs, it was Symington's. He selected his subjects, and if your malady did not appeal to him, well, that was too bad! He was utterly uninterested in you as a fellow human being – you were not on a level with *him*, good God no! The second difficulty was this: Symington *did* sometimes exact a fee. If there was a girl in the family, *she* would bear the cost. She might be sixteen, she might be fifteen. She was, on occasion, as young as twelve. The younger the better for Dr Symington. He was very discreet, and he never pushed his demands too hard, but you would be surprised at how often a desperate family considered such a fee worth paying for the life of a breadwinner. Symington was clever enough never to take his fee until after the operation, and then only if it had been successful. Then the girl would be sent to his rooms at the Medical School to, how shall I put it, express the family's gratitude. I know it seems monstrous, but these things happened.

'Well, I refilled Davie's glass and he put his head in his hands and said that if he had known then what he knew now, he would never have let Mary go. Symington operated on his sister, without success, but he had his fee, Mary, securely banked in Heriot Row. Away from her uncle's protection, Mary scrubbed floors and cleaned out fires, and was regularly debauched by her benefactor.'

'This is appalling,' I said. 'I never saw her there. I was only at the house twice, but . . .'

'Of course you didn't see her. You were in the drawing-room, she was below stairs, invisible to the likes of you.'

'But why did she not leave, especially once she knew her mother was dead?'

'To return to what? The grimmest of existences in the worst quarter of the city? She well knew how her uncle's friends made their living, and that she might shortly be reduced to the same occupation. She tholed Symington's assaults because, in spite of them, her life had improved.'

'How can you presume to say that?' I asked.

'Because she *told* me,' he said, and there was a sudden, passionate edge to his voice. 'She is a great philosopher, a stoic. She would bear almost anything so long as the promise of something better existed. But she had reckoned without Symington's ruthlessness. Three months ago or thereabouts, she was no longer able to conceal from him the condition to which his attentions had brought her. When he discovered it, he dismissed her from the house on the pretext that he had caught her pilfering the cutlery. He forbore to bring charges against her, and this pretended clemency, he hoped, would silence her. But Mary is made of sterner stuff than her meek exterior would suggest. She returned home and immediately told her uncle all that had happened.

'Davie, who, as I mentioned before, is an easy-going fellow when not defending the Empire or his family, was enraged. His first thought was to beat Symington to a pulp. His second was less noble, which only goes to show that moral expediency is not exclusive to the upper classes. He saw that he could profit from the situation, and that he might as well do so. He thought a spot of blackmail would earn him a pretty pound or two – with which, he told me, he had intended to make a new and better life for himself, his niece and her child. He waited a few weeks, and then demanded an interview with Symington at the

Medical School. Mary would soon give birth, he said. If the doctor did not pay a hefty sum in compensation, Davie would expose him, with the newborn child as evidence of his crime against a fifteen-year-old innocent.

'Symington bargained, reduced the price and received an assurance that uncle and niece would depart the country for ever. Davie, for his part, held out for a rendezvous on his own territory, and the deal was struck. The assignation was set, and the two men met on that wet, windy night nearly three weeks ago. But, Davie said, an argument began, because Symington had not brought the money. Davie had a knife with him for protection, and in a fit of rage, he claimed, he produced it and stabbed Symington several times. Then, full of remorse, he came straight to see me, bringing the doctor's bag. The fact that the bag was in his possession, he said, proved that he was the murderer, and that his motivation was theft.

'I said that in that case we had better look inside the bag, to see what was in it worth stealing. Davie became agitated. What did it matter what was in it? He'd committed homicide thinking it must contain something valuable. "I'll swing for it, Mr Cairncross," he said, "and the sooner the better."

'"Davie," I said, "I know you well enough to know that if you had been roused enough to kill Symington – and God knows you had sufficient reason – you would not regret it afterwards and you'd not be coming to me to assist you to the gallows. You're very keen to have me think you a murderer, Davie, but I'm telling you now, I won't let you stand up in court and say you killed a defenceless man for the contents of his medical bag. It's not good enough, my friend." He then tried to change tack, saying that he'd forgotten to mention that Symington was armed and had attacked him first, trying to stab him. I opened the bag and looked through the instruments it contained. The only item that might have been useful as a stabbing weapon was a large carving-knife with an ivory handle. I pulled it out. "Is this the weapon he used?" "Aye," Davie said rather too quickly. "Well, it certainly seems to be his," I said. "His initials are engraved on the blade. It has doubtless come from his house in Heriot Row. But I see he also cleaned it before he died," I went on. "How considerate of him! Unfortunately he missed this speck of blood on the handle, see? Are you injured, Davie?" He wasn't, of course. Then he gave that line up, and said that Symington hadn't had a weapon after all. "That brings us back to where we were before," I said, "and I still don't believe you killed him. But I'd be prepared to bet that this is his blood on the knife."

'Well, at this Davie quite broke down. "Ye're richt," he said, "I didna dae it. I dinna ken wha did, but I fear for them. O God, whit'll we dae, Mr Cairncross?"

'"We'll not panic, for a start," I told him. "Go home, destroy that shirt, and make sure there is nothing else to connect you – or Mary – with what has happened. Symington failed to bring the money with him, you say. Well, whether he did or didn't, the money is gone. It will do nobody any good now to mention it. Do you understand, Davie? The money need *never be mentioned again*." I am happy to say that, on this question at least, he did grasp my meaning.

'The next thing I told him to do was to look out for

berths on a ship going to some distant part of the Empire – to Canada, Australia or New Zealand, or to America. No doubt he and Mary could somehow scrape enough together for the passage. He nodded, catching my drift again. "Then," I said, "you must take the opportunity and go. There is nothing to be gained by staying, and only danger if you should somehow be connected with Symington's death." The one link, I said, was Mary's employment in the Heriot Row house. Did anyone else there – Mrs Symington, the butler, the cook? – know where Mary came from? No, Davie said, he was sure that they didn't. Symington had introduced her to the house, and nobody would have dared question his reasons for doing so. Then, I said, you should be able to leave without too much difficulty, so long as you go quickly.

'"The child is due tae gie birth at ony time," Davie protested. "We will go, but no until she is safely delivered." On this point, he absolutely refused to give way. I relented. You'll remember, that night in the howff, when I made sure Davie recognised your face? That was in case you were needed to deliver the bairn, for he would only allow near her a doctor whose competence and discretion I could vouch for. I knew I could trust you, and I believe you are a better doctor than you yourself think – you simply don't apply your skills where they are most needed. As it turned out, your services were not required. The two ladies of the night did sterling work as midwives, and last week, the day after Symington was buried, Mary gave birth to a healthy daughter.'

'She was there at the funeral,' I said. 'I saw her with my own eyes.'

'Aye, she told us she had been there, a most foolish act. I think, however, that it was necessary for her to see her abuser put into the earth. It released her in more ways than one. I have no doubt it brought on the birth. She rested for three days, and then, with my assistance, she and her uncle travelled to Greenock, boarded a ship there and are now several days into their voyage to . . . Ah, but it is probably better that I do not say where they have gone. Indeed, I do not know, except that they are bound for a new life in a foreign clime.'

'But this means,' I said, 'you have aided a murderer to escape justice.'

'Perhaps I have,' Cairncross said, without the least semblance of shame. 'I will never know, and nor will you or anyone else in Scotland. Do you mind you met me coming out of Blackfriars Wynd that Sunday after kirk? I had gone to satisfy myself there was no evidence at the scene of the murder that might lead the authorities to Khyber Davie. I was determined I would not see a man hanged for a crime he had not committed. As for justice, I think it was done three weeks ago.'

'You contradict yourself,' I said. 'If you believe Khyber Davie to be innocent, you had no need to check for clues that might incriminate him. You must *know* he was not the murderer.'

'That is correct,' he said, eyeing me steadily. 'As I said, justice has been done.'

'Not for Mrs Symington and her daughters,' I protested. 'I hear they will have to leave Heriot Row and go to the country, to fall on the charity of some cousin or other. Who will marry either of those graceless daughters now, knowing in all probability they will have to take on the widow as well? And – because of *your* actions – they will never see anyone brought to justice for the murder of their parent and spouse.'

'The greater injustice,' he said, quite unperturbed by my objections, 'would have been to allow another human to be killed to compensate them for the loss. You can denounce me if you wish, but it will do no good. I will deny everything, and there is absolutely no evidence to support any accusations of guilt against Davie you might care to make.'

'It might not be Davie I accuse,' I said. 'What about the medical bag? And the carving-knife, which I presume was *pilfered* from Heriot Row?'

'What about them?' Cairncross said. 'They will never be found.' He spoke with conviction, and I knew that he himself must have disposed of them.

'Then why have you told me all this?' I asked, feeling a thrill of pleasure that he had thus taken me into his confidence, and knowing that he was right – that I would not betray it.

'Because I like you,' he said, 'for all your faults. I think if you had been in my shoes you would not have acted so very differently. And now, why don't you fetch over that decanter? I find after all this talk that my throat is a little dry.'

Monday 29th November

Today saw the passing of Lady Balcathro. I have spent the last four days constantly at her bedside, and she was bright almost to the end. Until Saturday she regaled me with wonderfully bloodthirsty tales of the resurrectionists, which she assured me were the undiluted truth. Then she began to fail, and so, in order to take her mind off her pain – and in order to relieve myself of a burning desire to tell *somebody* – I took my turn and recounted a complicated tale of murder and vengeance, involving a certain *sleekit* doctor, a man with one eye, a lawyer with an ambivalent attitude to the law, a wronged lassie and a couple of strumpets – all of it, I said, as true as her own narratives. Lady B. enjoyed every detail she heard, and I enjoyed those she slept through. She always was capable of the utmost discretion when it mattered, and has now taken my story with her to the grave. I am convinced that no other physician could have made her passage from this life more comfortable.

And now I am at the start of a fresh phase of my own life. I will – I must – turn over a new leaf. If I start making resolutions now, I will have no excuses come the New Year. I have, for example, scarcely touched a drop of alcohol this last week, and feel I will sleep like a baby tonight.

I have never had a repetition of that nightmare. But as I sat beside Lady B.'s bed and she slumbered, sometimes pictures flashed unbidden before me, of young Mary, demure and placid beside her uncle in the howff, or standing at a distance at the funeral, just as if she were there to make sure everything was done in the proper fashion. There was something quite disconcerting about her calmness, and yet perhaps it was this that enabled her to overcome the things that happened to her, and that will see her stand steadfast against future tribulations. I cannot but wish her well – and her daughter, and Khyber

Davie – wherever they make landfall. I would not, however, advise any man even to consider taking advantage of her, not if he values his life.

As for Charlie Cairncross, I have not seen him for two weeks. I still do not know exactly who or what he is, but I do wonder at his extraordinary devotion to Davie and his niece, which so greatly surpassed any small loyalty he might have had for the old soldier. I wonder too at his great efficiency in getting rid of evidence, not least the ivory-handled carving-knife. Such dedication! A man prepared to go to such lengths, I feel, would do almost anything to achieve his ends.

Dead Close

LIN ANDERSON

Doug Cameron stared wide-eyed into the darkness, his heart racing, fear prickling his skin. The dream. As fresh now as it had been seventeen years ago. For a few moments Rebecca was alive, the swell of her pregnancy as clear as her terrified expression, then she was running from him as though he was the source of her fear.

A police siren wailed past in tune with his thoughts, its blue light flickering his rain-splattered window. He rose and went to watch the squad car's progress, leaning against the window frame, reminding himself that in 48 hours that sound would belong to his past. Just like the view from the bedroom window. Just like Rebecca.

When he felt steadier, he went through to the kitchen and began the process of making coffee, glancing at the photograph on the fridge door as he fetched out the milk carton. He'd taken the picture from the garden of his future home. A view of the flat-topped slopes of Duncaan on the Island of Raasay instead of Edinburgh Castle. Not a bad exchange, he decided.

Cameron settled at the kitchen table, pulled over his work box and began the intricate task of tying a new fishing fly. The only thing that helped him forget the dream, and the past.

Detective Sergeant James Boyd woke with a start. Immediately, his body reacted to its cramped position on the sofa, sending waves of pain through his knees and lower back.

Boyd wasn't sure which noise had wakened him, the screaming baby or his mobile. Through the open bedroom door he could see Bev put their young son to the breast, silencing his cries. Boyd answered the duty officer in monosyllables, pulling on his trousers and shirt as he did so. He turned, sensing Bev in the doorway. She looked pointedly at him.

'I have to go to work.'

Bev said nothing, but her expression was the same as always. Tired, resentful, desperate.

'I'm sorry,' he tried.

'Will Susan be there?' she said sharply.

Boyd covered guilt with irritation. 'She's forensic. If there's a crime, she's there.'

Bev turned on her heel, Rory still attached to her breast. The last thing Boyd saw before the bedroom door banged shut was a small chubby hand clutching the air.

When his phone rang, Cameron contemplated ignoring it. The only call he would get at this time was one he didn't want.

'Glad you're up, Sir.' His Detective Sergeant's voice was suspiciously cheery. 'We've had a call out.'

'I've retired,' Cameron tried.

'Not till Tuesday,' Boyd reminded him.

Cameron listened in silence to the details. A serious incident had been reported at Greyfriars Churchyard, a stone's throw from his flat.

'I'll walk round,' he offered.

'No need, Sir. I'll be with you in five minutes.'

Cameron wondered if Boyd suspected he wouldn't come otherwise.

Boyd's car stank of stale vinegar, the door pocket stuffed with fish and chip wrappers, a sure sign he wasn't eating at home. His DS looked rough; stubble-faced and bleary-eyed.

'How's the new arrival?' Cameron asked.

'Only happy when he's attached to Bev's tit.'

'A typical male then.'

Boyd attempted a smile. Cameron thought about adding something, like 'Hang on in there. Things'll get better', but didn't know if that was true.

They were at the graveyard in minutes, sweeping past the statue of Greyfriars Bobby and through the gates of the ancient churchyard. Ahead, the pale edifice that was the church loomed out of an early morning mist.

A couple of uniforms stood aside to let the two men enter the mausoleum; one of many that lined the walls of the graveyard. Inside, the air was musty and chill. The light-headed feeling Cameron had experienced earlier returned, and he reached out to steady himself against the doorframe, bowing his head to relieve the sudden pressure between his eyes. The beam from Boyd's high-powered torch played over the interior, finally settling on a pool of fresh blood next to a stone casket.

'The caller reported seeing a figure run in through the gate. Then they heard a woman scream.'

Cameron said nothing. He wanted to make it plain that if Boyd expected to take over as DI, this was the time to start.

'We've done an initial search of the graveyard. Nothing so far. And no blood except in here.'

Cameron registered the oddity of this, but made no

comment. He didn't want to be drawn in. He didn't want his brain to focus on anything other than his departure.

They emerged to find a parked forensic van and two SOCOs getting kitted up. Cameron watched as Boyd and the young woman exchanged looks. He walked out of hearing, not wanting to be party to something he couldn't prevent. Besides, what could he say? Don't piss on your wife or you could end up like me?

He had no idea what made him look up. The medieval stone tenement behind him merged with the back wall of the crypt. It was blank-faced, except for one narrow window. The young woman who watched him was in shadow but Cameron briefly made out a pale face and long dark hair, before she stepped out of sight.

It took him five minutes to circumnavigate the building and gain entry. The internal stairwell spiralled swiftly from ground level, one door on each floor. He climbed to the second landing and knocked.

When the young woman opened the door, Cameron's voice froze in his throat.

Cameron had been a detective long enough to read body language pretty accurately. Susan was on her knees on the muddy grass, Boyd trying hard not to look at her upturned buttocks. He stood to attention when he spotted Cameron. Another sign.

'I spoke to a girl living up there,' Cameron pointed at the window. 'She says she was wakened by the siren. Didn't see or hear anything before that.'

Boyd gave him an odd look. Cameron wasn't planning to say the girl looked so like Rebecca it'd almost given him a heart attack, but wondered if the shock still showed on his face.

'Well the police dog was right. It is a grave, but not a fresh one.' Susan sat back to reveal a sunken area in the muddy trampled grass. 'They buried plague victims here in medieval times. There were so many it raised the ground level by twenty feet. Heavy rain sometimes washes the top soil away, exposing the remains.'

Cameron stepped closer, his eye caught by a glint of metal.

'What's that?'

Susan fished it out and wiped off the mud. 'Looks like a brooch.' She handed it over.

Cameron felt the prick as the pin caught his thumb. Blood oozed from the wound to form a red bubble. The sight of it made him nauseous.

'The plague bacteria are way out of date,' Susan quipped, 'but I'd renew your tetanus if I were you.' She slipped the brooch into an evidence bag. 'I should have something for you on the blood in the crypt in twenty-four hours.'

'That's Boyd's department now,' Cameron told her.

He left them to it, giving the excuse of packing to cover his early departure. The truth was, in his head he was no longer a policeman. Thirty-five years of detective work had come and gone and the city was no better or safer now than when he'd begun. Worse than that, the dream this morning and the young woman he'd spoken to in the flat above the graveyard had only served to remind Cameron that the one case he should have solved, he never had.

*

It wasn't much for a lifetime. Cameron surveyed the meagre group of boxes. Everything had been packed except the books. There wasn't much shelf space at the cottage. He would have to be ruthless.

He started well, splitting the books into two piles, one for Cancer Research, the other destined for Raasay. There were at least half a dozen on fly fishing, all of which went on the Raasay pile. The last book on the shelf was one about Edinburgh's past. Cameron recognised it as belonging to Rebecca. Not a native to the city, she'd taken an amused interest in its medieval history, both fact and fiction. The photograph fell out as he transferred the book to the Raasay pile.

Rebecca stood by a dark expanse of water, laughing as she tried to anchor her long dark hair against the wind. On the lapel of her jacket she wore a brooch. Cameron suddenly remembered buying her the brooch from a silversmith near Glendale as a birthday present – a swirling Celtic pattern, not unlike the one they'd found in the ancient grave.

The flashback had all the power and detail of the original event. Rebecca standing next to the counter, her head bowed as she examined the selection. He could even smell her perfume as she turned to show him which one she'd chosen.

Cameron sat down heavily, his legs like water. This was how it had been when she'd first disappeared. The powerful, terrible dreams; the intensity of her presence. The fear that she was in danger and he couldn't save her.

He had no idea how long he sat there, unmoving, before he heard the buzzer.

★

Boyd stood awkwardly amidst the packing cases. Cameron thought again how much he liked his DS. He wanted to tell Boyd he would make a good Inspector but he shouldn't let the job take over his life. Instead, Cameron said nothing.

He'd laid the Edinburgh book on the Raasay pile. Boyd picked it up, checked out the cover and flicked through a few pages. Cameron was aware his DS was stalling for time. There was something he wanted to say, but didn't know how.

'You don't believe in all this stuff, Sir?'

'What stuff?'

'Ghosts?'

Boyd's eyes were shadowed from lack of sleep. The pregnancy, Cameron gathered, had been unplanned. The timing wasn't good for him or Bev, Boyd had said. Cameron suddenly recalled his own reaction when Rebecca had told him she was pregnant. The worry and confusion mingled with his desire to say the right thing.

'We're all haunted, one way or another, Sergeant.' Cameron handed Boyd the photograph. 'This is Rebecca, my wife, taken just before she went missing. Look at the brooch she's wearing.'

Boyd studied the picture. 'That's what I came about, Sir. We've found something I think you should see.'

On the way, Cameron had this expectant feeling. It was something he'd experienced countless times on the job, the breakthrough moment, when the pieces of the jigsaw fell into place.

An incident tent had been raised over the plague pit.

A foot below the surface they'd exposed a mummified body. Cameron could make out strands of long dark hair.

'There's a lot of sandy soil in this section,' Susan was saying. 'It leeched the fluids from the body. That's why it's preserved. The brooch must have been attached to the clothes.'

Cameron's heart was in his mouth. 'How long has it been there?'

'At a guess a couple of decades,' Susan avoided his eye.

Cameron stared into the grave. Was it possible that this could be Rebecca? That all the time she'd been buried here, half a mile from her home?

He recalled with utmost clarity the morning he'd returned from work to find the flat empty, Rebecca gone. She'd been tearful when he'd been called out the previous night. The pregnancy had made her vulnerable – something he'd resented, because it made his life difficult. Cameron still felt guilty at the relief he'd experienced when the door had closed on the sound of her distress.

The months following her disappearance had been hell. He'd been in charge of missing person cases himself; interviewed husbands about their wives, known the statistics that pointed to the partner as the prime suspect. He'd had to endure the same accusations himself.

It had all ended nowhere. No Rebecca, no body. And all the time Cameron had hoped she'd simply left him. That they were both alive somewhere, Rebecca and the child. This morning when the girl opened the door, her extraordinary likeness to Rebecca, for a moment he'd hoped . . .

'The girl in the flat. Have you spoken to her?'

The look he'd seen earlier was back on Boyd's face.

'The flat's unoccupied, Sir.'

'Nonsense. I spoke to a young woman. She looked like . . .' Cameron stopped himself.

'According to the neighbours, the flat's been empty for months, Sir.'

Cameron took the stairs two at a time. He was already banging on the door when Boyd caught him up. Boyd let him go through the process three times, before he intervened.

'There's no one there, Sir.'

'I saw her, Sergeant.' Cameron was pissed off by Boyd's expression. He might be about to retire, but he wasn't senile yet. Cameron put his shoulder to the door.

The room was empty – of everything. For a terrible moment Cameron thought the dream that haunted his nights had somehow spilled over into the day. The fantasy of Rebecca being alive, of the child surviving, had fuelled his daytime imagination. But why here? Why now?

Boyd was standing silently in the doorway.

Cameron pushed past, suddenly desperate to be out of that room.

'I don't see how that's possible.' Boyd looked again at the DNA results. Anyone working with the police had their DNA taken and stored on the database. It was routine. Susan's tests on the blood traces in the crypt had come up with two types. One matched the boss, the other was an unknown.

'There must have been contamination when the samples were taken,' Boyd insisted.

Susan was adamant. 'The only way for this to happen is for him to have bled in that room.'

'He cut his finger on the brooch,' he tried in desperation.

'That was afterwards.'

Boyd was at a complete loss. He would have to bring Cameron in, ask him how the hell his blood got in that crypt. Boyd didn't relish the thought.

'What about the body?' he asked.

'Tests are ongoing. Superficially it's the same build as Rebecca, but what's left of the clothes suggest it may be older. We're checking the teeth against Rebecca's dental records. The brooch is the only real match and it's not unique.'

Boyd had pulled the file on Rebecca's disappearance and spent most of the previous night reading it. Seventeen years ago he hadn't even joined the force, so anything he'd heard about the boss's missing wife was hearsay. Boyd wished he'd read the story sooner. It would have explained a lot about the old man.

He thought about the last few weeks, the boss's odd behaviour. Boyd knew he hadn't been sleeping. The DI had made a joke of it, suggesting it was excitement at getting out at last, but Boyd suspected that wasn't the real reason.

He flicked through the well-thumbed documents in the file. There were transcripts of at least six interviews with Cameron.

'What if the boss did have something to do with his wife's disappearance?'

Susan looked unconvinced. 'Why? There was nothing wrong between them. No evidence of an affair . . .' she halted mid-sentence.

A sick feeling anchored itself in the pit of Boyd's stomach. He had a sudden image of life repeating itself. The same stupid people doing the same stupid things.

'Susan . . .'

She held up her hand to stop him. 'Don't.'

The Royal Mile hummed with life in the late summer light. Cameron passed the usual mix of street artists and musicians circled by enthusiastic tourists. Near the Mercat Cross a young woman was regaling a group with stories of Edinburgh's past. Cameron checked the nearby advertising boards for city tours.

The poster he sought had been on the wall of the flat. He'd spotted it when the girl opened the door. An advert for a ghost tour, one of several that roamed the old city, above and below ground. Like many Edinburghers, Cameron had left that sort of thing to the tourists. *Dead Close.* Had he imagined the poster in the same way he'd imagined the girl?

He spotted a board for a ghost tour of Greyfriars Churchyard with a cancelled notice stuck across it. There was nothing advertising *Dead Close.*

In the end, he found it by chance. Later, Cameron would recall the entrance, remember it as the one in his dream, yet knowing there were scores of such archways lining the Royal Mile.

A young man wearing a long black cloak was calling a group to order outside a heavy wooden door, asking who among them was willing to cross the threshold of *Dead Close*.

The passageway was narrow, low and rough underfoot, dropping steeply. Cameron knew of Underground Edinburgh, the bowels of the older city beneath its current counterpart, but had never visited it before. He was fascinated by the narrow stone passageway, the small cell-like rooms to either side. It was bare and clean now, but the squalor in medieval times must have been horrendous. No wonder plague had broken out here.

The tour guide had brought them to a halt, encouraging the group to view one of the rooms. Cameron took his place at the back. The guide was telling the story of a child, separated from its mother when plague broke out and the city authorities quarantined the Close.

Cameron wasn't shocked by the story, but by the room. Rough shelves housed a multitude of toys and sweets left by visitors who'd professed to sense the ghost-child's loneliness. Cameron turned away, irritated by the guide's tone, no longer willing to be part of this make-believe. It was then he saw the doll, wedged in the corner, three shelves up.

'We're not supposed to touch the presents.'

Cameron showed him his ID card. The guide lifted the doll down and handed it over. A ripple of excitement moved through the group. They were wondering if this was for real or just part of the tour. Cameron examined the doll. It looked just like the one he'd seen on the window seat in the flat, one eye dropped in its socket, the blue dress faded.

'I believe a young woman may have left this here. She was in her late teens, long dark hair?'

The guide looked blank. He must have taken scores of people round this place. 'Wait a minute. There was a girl, a couple of nights ago. She joined just as we came in. I wasn't sure she'd paid, but I decided to let it go.'

'Did she give a name?'

The guide shook his head.

This wasn't fucking real. Boyd shifted his feet, discomfort showing in every inch of his body. Across the table, the old man looked calm. Boyd tried to work out what he was thinking and couldn't. Had it been anyone else, the interview would have been formal.

'You've never been in there before that night?'

Cameron shook his head.

'Then how did traces of your blood get on the scene, Sir?'

'I have no idea.'

Jesus, he didn't want this to end up as an investigation into an officer contaminating a scene of crime. Boyd contemplated keeping quiet about it, at least until the boss handed in his badge.

Cameron looked impatient, as though he had no interest in the fact that his blood had been found in the crypt.

'What about the body? Is it Rebecca?'

Boyd hesitated. The tests weren't complete yet, but there was no point keeping the old man thinking they'd found his dead wife. He shook his head. 'Forensic think it's much older.'

Cameron gave a small nod as though he wasn't surprised.

'The girl I met in the flat looked like Rebecca. Our daughter would have been her age by now. Rebecca had an old-fashioned doll that was hers as a kid. It was the only thing missing from the house when she left.'

Boyd's heart was sinking fast. He didn't want the old man to go on, but couldn't bring himself to stop him.

Cameron produced a china-faced doll in a faded blue dress. One eye hung low in its socket.

Something cold crawled up Boyd's spine.

Cameron's eyes were bright with excitement. 'The girl I spoke to had this doll in the flat. There was a poster on the wall. It advertised a ghost tour called *Dead Close*. I took that tour. There's a room dedicated to a child ghost. This doll was on the shelf.'

Cameron was staring at him, waiting for Boyd to respond.

What the hell was he supposed to say? That he'd had the flat searched again, even had Susan go over it forensically. That she'd been adamant no one had set foot in it for months. That this girl the DI kept going on about didn't exist, except in his imagination.

Pity engulfed Boyd. Thirty-five years of service, on the point of retirement, and the old man had lost it.

Cameron wandered down the Royal Mile, silent and deserted in the dark hours before dawn. It was the time he liked best. The right time to say goodbye. Without people, cars and lights, the city felt like his alone.

Boyd had humoured him. Organised a search for the mysterious girl but, apart from the tour guide, no one had professed to seeing her. The other occupants of the tenement continued to insist the flat had lain empty for months.

So he'd imagined it all; conjured up a daughter who didn't exist? Cameron could have accepted that, had it not been for the doll.

The rain had come on, beating heavily on his head and shoulders. Cameron was impervious to it, his gaze fastened on the arch leading to *Dead Close*. The Royal Mile had grown darker under the sudden downpour, the space around him airless, making it difficult to breathe. Cameron leaned against the stone wall, his legs suddenly weak.

He watched as a figure emerged from the archway opposite. The figure turned towards him, the swell of her pregnancy suddenly visible.

'Rebecca?'

The figure turned, and for a moment Cameron believed she recognised him. A sob rose in his throat. Then she was off, hurrying up the steep cobbles of the Mile, turning left towards Greyfriars.

Cameron ran like he had never run before, yet always her fleeing figure was the same distance ahead. Fear drove him forward. He knew this time he must catch her up, or else lose her for ever.

He reached the Greyfriars gate, his breath rasping in his throat, his heart crashing. Ahead, the door of the mausoleum lay open. Cameron slithered across the rain-soaked grass and stood at the crypt door.

'Rebecca?' he called.

The moon broke through the cloud, dropping a faint line of light on the stone casket. Cameron could see nothing but that line of light yet every nerve and fibre of his body told him someone was in there and that they could hear him.

He poured out his heart to the darkness and shadows. He loved her. He should never have left her alone that night. He should never have stopped searching.

He fell silent as a figure stepped from behind the casket. Cameron called out Rebecca's name, but the woman wasn't looking at him but at someone else.

The shadow of a male loomed against the wall, then took form. Words were exchanged between them. Words that Cameron did not understand. His own voice was silenced, his body frozen in time.

The woman screamed and launched herself at the man. Cameron heard a grunt of surprise then saw him crumble and fall. Blood pooled at Cameron's feet. He looked round in vain for its source, for there was no longer anyone there but him.

Boyd steeled himself and went inside the flat. Packing cases were stacked neatly in the hallway, each one with its contents detailed on the side. Two fishing rods stood upright in the corner.

He hesitated before pushing open the sitting room door. The place was empty. Boyd chose the kitchen next. He had been in this room many times. It was where the DI liked to sit. From the window, the Castle stood resolute against the sky. Cameron's tin box sat open on the table, a part-assembled fishing fly nearby.

Boyd listened outside the bedroom door. Maybe the old man was fast asleep? Praying wasn't something Boyd did, but he made an exception as he pushed open that door.

Cameron was lying fully clothed on top of the bed. For a moment, Boyd thought he was sleeping. The Edinburgh book lay open on his chest. The doll he'd pestered Boyd about sat in the crook of his arm. Blood running from his nostrils, eyes and ears had caked on his face and neck.

The book was just one of many that told the story of Edinburgh's haunted places. Most of the stories were invented. This one was no different. Boyd read the passage the boss had circled.

The mausoleum is haunted by the ghost of the man responsible for quarantining Dead Close. He was killed by the mother of a child he'd walled in to die. The authorities executed the woman and she was buried in a mass grave with other plague victims. Visitors have reported seeing a pool of blood on the floor of the mausoleum and hearing the woman scream.

Boyd closed the book and slipped it in a drawer of his filing cabinet. Whatever it said, he didn't believe in ghosts.

Blood, on the other hand, was real.

They'd had no luck trying to find the person who'd bled in the crypt. As for the boss's contribution – that was the warning they'd all missed.

Boyd wondered if the boss knew his life had sat on a knife edge. Maybe that was why he'd made up the story of the girl – the daughter he'd never had. Perhaps the old man just wanted one last chance to make things right.

The pathology report had stated that the brain aneurysm that killed Cameron had been developing for some time. He would have experienced all the symptoms: light-headedness, rapid heartbeat, nose bleeds and finally a massive drop in blood pressure as it burst.

Detective Inspector Boyd sat for a minute in the darkness of his office. Everyone else had gone. He picked up the phone and called home. After a few moments Bev answered.

'What's wrong?'

'Nothing,' Boyd said, happy just to hear her voice.

Bev lay on her right side, her swollen breasts leaking through the T-shirt. She was sound asleep, her breath coming in small puffs. Boyd went to the cot and looked in at the other male in Bev's life, the one who had stolen those breasts. The lips were puckered from sucking, eyes moving behind blue lids.

'I know what you're dreaming about,' Boyd whispered.

The eyes flickered open, a tiny fist thrust the air. Bev stirred in response as though the two were still attached, umbilical cord unbroken.

Boyd offered his finger. At his touch, the fist fastened round him. Boyd was amazed at its strength.

He undressed and got into bed, gathering his wife in his arms. Bev pressed against him, damp, smelling of milk. Boyd kissed her hair, her eyes, her mouth.

Chris Takes The Bus

DENISE MINA

They stood outside the plate glass window at the bus station, because inside was so bright and cheerful, so full of happy milling people, that neither could bear it.

The cold was channelled here, into a snaking stream that lapped at their ankles, a bitter snapping cold that chilled them both. His eyes were fixed on the ground and she could feel him shrinking, sinking into the concrete.

'Jees-ho!' She shivered theatrically, trying to bring his attention back to her.

Chris looked at her and pulled the zip up at his neck, making a defiant face that said, see? I can look after myself, I know to do my coat up against the cold. They were huddled in their coats, shoulders up at their ears, each alone.

He tried to smile at her but she glanced down at the bag on the floor because his eyes were so hard to look into. The backlit adverts tinged the ground an icy pink and she saw that Chris had put the heel of his bag in a puddle.

'Bag's getting soggy,' she smiled nervously, keeping her eyes averted.

He looked at it, dismayed at yet another fuck-up, and then shrugged, shaking his head a little, as if trying to shake off the concern she must be feeling. 'Dry out on the bus.'

She nodded, 'Yeah, it'll get hot in there.'

'Phew,' he looked away down the concrete fairway.

'Last time I only had a T-shirt and jeans on and I was sweating like a menopausal woman.'

His turn of phrase made her mouth twitch.

'When I got off I had salt rings under my arms.'

She tutted disbelievingly.

'True,' he insisted. 'I stood still at King's Cross and a couple of deer came up and licked me.'

She smirked away from him, felt her eyes brimming up at the same time and frowned to cover it up.

'One of them offered me a tenner for a gobble, actually.'

She was crying and laughing at the same time, spluttering ridiculously, the pink glow from the adverts glinting off her wet cheeks. His whole fucking venture depended on a lie and she wasn't a good liar.

'So,' she wiped her face and turned back to him, 'so when you get there you're off to –'

'My Auntie Margie's, yeah.' He had done her the courtesy of looking away, giving her the chance to get it together before he looked back. 'Yeah, she'll be waiting in for me, got my room ready.'

'D'you get on with her?'

Chris shrugged, 'She's my auntie . . .'

He tipped gently forward on his heels, leaning out into the brutal wind beyond the shelter. A coach pulled past the mouth of the bus station, slowly, dim yellow lights behind the shaded windows. They both saw the rabbit-ear side mirrors. It was a luxury coach, luxury in as much as coaches ever could be. Full of fat tourists coming to see the Castle and the Mile, the pantomime of the city. Not the London Bus, not Chris's bus.

He stepped back and they watched the bus pass, heads swinging around in unison like a pair of kittens watching a ball swing in front of them.

'I'll not get that one,' he said, joking that he had a choice. 'I'll just wait for the shit bus and get that one.'

'Yeah,' she said cheerfully, and looking up saw him flinch, arcing his head back as his neck stiffened. He was still bleeding, she knew, had asked her if it was showing through the seat of his jeans, made her look. It wasn't showing. She'd given him a fanny pad to put down there and he joked about having a period. She didn't know who'd raped him, but it was someone they both knew, or else he wouldn't be leaving. He confided in her because she was mousey, would give him the money for the ticket without asking too much detail, wouldn't make him go to the police.

It came suddenly, a hot molten gush of dread from the base of her gut, rolling up her chest until it bubbled and burst out of her mouth: 'Don't go.' Her voice was flat and loud, ridiculous, a voice from the middle of a heated argument.

Chris looked at her, eyebrows tented pitifully. 'I have tae . . .'

She nodded, looked away.

'I have,' he whispered. 'Have to. You'll come and visit me.'

'Of course. Of course, and we'll phone all the time.'

'Yeah, phone. We'll phone.'

As a coach slowly eased its way around the sharp turn into the St Andrew Bus Station, the destination lit up brightly above the windscreen.

The passengers who had waited inside, in the warm, filtered out behind them, talking excitedly, swinging bags, forming a messy queue.

Conscious of the company, Chris shifted his weight, brushing her shoulder lightly, shifting away. She felt the loss quite suddenly, a wrench, another cherished friend swallowed by the promise of London, loading the coach boot with bags stuffed with the offal of their own history.

As God Made Us

A.L. KENNEDY

Dan never explained why he woke up so early, or what it was that made him leave the flat. Folk wouldn't get it if he told them, so he didn't tell. He'd just head off out there and be ready for the pre-light, the dayshine you could see at around four a.m. – something about four at this point in the year – he'd be under that, stood right inside it. Daily. Without fail. Put on the soft shoes, jersey, tracky bottoms and the baseball cap and then off down the stairs to his street. His territory. Best to think of it as his – this way it was welcoming and okay.

He'd lean on the railings by number six and listen and settle his head, control it, and watch the glow start up from the flowers someone had planted in these big round-bellied pots, ceramic pots with whole thick fists of blossom in them now: a purple kind and a crimson, and both shades luminous, really almost sore with brightness, especially when all else was still dim. They only needed a touch of dawn and they'd kick off, raging. Dan liked them. Loved them. He would be sorry when they went away.

Since the birds would be more of a constant, he made sure he loved them as well: their first breaks of song across the softness, the caution and beauty in signals that hid their location, became vague and then faded as you closed on them. He thought there was almost nothing so fine as feeling their secrets pass round him and do no harm and he'd let himself wish to pick out the notes with his fingers like smooth, hot stones: little pebbles with a glimmer he could easily hold, could picture putting in his pockets, saving them. He'd imagine they might rattle when he walked: his weight landing and swinging and landing in the way it did, the only way it could, providing enough clumsiness to jolt them. Or maybe they'd call out again when they took a knock, maybe that would happen. In his head, anything could happen – it was freedom in there: big horizons and fine possibilities, that kind of shite – and chirping whenever he moved would be nice. So Dan would have it. He'd insist.

The other noises Dan could do without – there were too many of them and they were too much. They came in at him off the bare walls in his new digs, rebounded and propagated amongst the landlord's efforts at furniture. He'd to put up with clatters and small impacts – perhaps impacts – and vehicles – engines, metalsounds – and shouting and murmuring: voices that might be planning, that could have a bad intent, and footfalls: creeping, dashes, jogging. Fox screams were the worst – they sounded like bone pain and being lost, losing. And, caught in the house, you could not assess your situation, could neither prepare nor react – you were held in an impossible state.

Being caught at the railings wasn't as bad. Standing there you would realise that you were naked: no cover, no defence: and so you would send a ghost of yourself running down to the basement door – send this piece from your thoughts that would chase and then lie out flat in the shadows you've seen at the foot of the steps. It could hide there, your will between it and any harm. It could even curl up like a child, like a hiding boy, while you mother it, father it, let it be secure. The rest of you, which was the part that was real and existed and knew what's appropriate: *that* part could stay where it was and be firm – nothing going wrong – and could appreciate a mercy was taking place, a chance of survival all over again, and a measure to show your recovery's success.

This kind of trick in his thinking was needed because, as had been previously and very often discussed with professionals of several kinds, he was a brave bastard – the brave bastards being the ones who were shitting themselves and did what they had to, anyway.

He managed.

He'd begun to use earplugs when it was night. He'd be snug in his pit by ten and the covers up over his head – which made him hot, but then again he'd been hotter and covers up over would let him sleep – and the plugs would be in and packing his skull with the racket of being alive: swallowing and a background thrum – like he had engines and they were running – and his breath pacing back and forth and keeping as restless as you'd want it, keeping on.

Sometimes the press of the foam would make his ears hurt, or start to tickle, but that he could tolerate. Putting in the right one was very slightly awkward. Could be worse, though – could be having to sew on a button as part of his personal maintenance, or peeling potatoes, or that whole process of taking a crap – which, these days, he really noticed how often he did, even though he'd cut back on eating potatoes, obviously – except for chips from the chipper, from *Frying Tonite*, which were made by either Doris, or Steve who was her other son, the one who wasn't dead. Those things were ticklish tasks. They were interesting challenges in his reconstructed life. They were fucking pains in the arse.

When he's together with the lads he doesn't much mention such details because they are obvious and aren't important, not like they seem when he's alone.

'Oh, the many, many pains in young Daniel's delicate arse . . . But on the other hand . . .'

'On the other hand – Aaw . . . look, I dropped it.'

'Well, fucking pick it up again, hands are expensive.'

Once every month they swim together: six gentlemen sharing a leisurely day. They choose whoever's turn it is to be host, fire off the emails, travel however far, and then rendezvous at a swimming baths and christen The Gathering.

They call it that because of the movies with the Highlander in, the ones with everybody yelling at each other – *There can be only one.* – and mad, immortal buggers slicing each other's heads off with these massive swords.

You have only got the one head and shouldn't lose it.

For this Gathering they'll do the usual: swimming in the morning and then a big lunch and then getting pissed and then going back to Gobbler's place, because this was his turn, and eating all his scran and some carryout and then watching DVDs of their films and getting more pissed and maybe some porn and maybe not. They'd tried going to clubs in the early days – strip clubs, lap dancing – and one night in Aberdeen they'd gone to a neat, wee semi full of prossies – foreign prossies in fact, prossies from Moldova – but that never worked out too well. Porn was better sometimes.

In the baths everything is standard, predictable, doesn't

matter what pool they come to. First there's the push or the pull on heavy doors and that walk into a punch of hot air – stuns your breath a bit – and then chlorine smell and kiddie smell and there'll be that sense of a space nearby, light and high with the huge tearing windows – the windows will take out at least the one wall – and all of that water trapped underneath the airiness, that pressure and weight.

Dan and the others, they'll start mucking about, getting wound up by the anticipation of effort – flailing themselves from once place to another, hither and yon – the idea of fitness, applicable force – and more mucking about.

'Hey! Salt and vinegar!' Gobbler is shouting at Dan. Gobbler with an accent that is East of Scotland and Dan who sounds West – sounds, he supposes, like he's from Coatbridge, because he is. Gobbler is from salt and sauce land and Dan is from salt and vinegar. On occasion, they set out the subtleties of this to the others.

'Gobbler's from the heathen side – they put salt and sauce on their chips.'

'Jock bastards – everything comes back to chips with you – not even fish and chips, just chips.' Frank dodges in with this, yelling – sounds like he's near to Gobbler, out of sight behind a row of changing cubicles. 'How long are you meant to live, anyway, on fried Mars bars and bloody chips?'

'About till we're twenty.' Dan remembers the trip they had to Kettering – which is where Frank has settled. It's a wee, grey hoor of a place. 'Twenty years in Kettering, that'd feel like eighty. I'd top myself.'

The lot of them of them shouting back and forth at

each other, scattered in the room, while they change and are over-excited and Dan thinks of being at school and how that was: swimming days with rubbish pals – pals who weren't pals at all – and not wanting to get undressed, being scared that he'd maybe sink this time, choke, scared of standing in nothing but trunks and somebody picking him out, starting something, having a go, and then the teachers coming in to the troublemakers and saying they had to behave and this being a relief to Dan, but also shaming – he knew it wasn't right, that he should sort his own problems, but couldn't. He'd been shy then and not aware of his potential and people could miss things in children – this happens constantly, he's certain – and even if an adult might try to be helpful, they might not do it a good way. Not enough care is taken. He worries for kids quite often. He wonders how they get through. He is extremely concerned that each possible kid should get through. He considers doing voluntary work with youngsters.

Dan as a youngster, he'd got his head down and tried to be correct, quiet and correct, tucked himself out of sight inside the rules. It was two years back, three, since he'd left that stuff – such a long while. He'd not forgotten, though – how he'd been pathetic.

Gobbler is hammering on the lockers between him and Dan and asking, bellowing, 'You got your kit off yet?' Gobbler who had another name in other times and places, when he was with other Gobblers, but now he is by himself and not in a regiment, so he is *the* Gobbler – he is the representative of his type. '*Oh, Danny Boy* . . . You having trouble?'

No one will come in and tell them they have to do anything today. They will misbehave.

'Piss off.'

'Your pants are removed over the feet, remember – not over the head. Poor bloody Paras, you do get confused.'

'Fuck off.'

And they are none of them pathetic.

'Are you naked yet, though, Danny? Getting hard just thinking about it.' Gobbler rattles something that sounds metallic and laughs. 'And here's old Fez, living up to his name . . . a dapper and fragrant man. Your heady aroma, sir, reminds me of those lovely evenings back at the mess when I ran the naked bar.'

A few strangers are in here too, but they are minding their own business. Mostly. Dan catches one of them giving him a walty look: flirty mix of interest and disgust, something that likes being almost scared, but wouldn't want the whole real deal, not a bit. Dan stares at him while shouting back to Gobbler, shouting hard so that spittle leaves him, so that his heartbeat wakes.

'Bollocks!'

'Exactly. And where there's bollocks . . .'

'Don't start.'

'There's the mighty Gobbler javelin of spam. You know when I get hard now –'

Everyone joining in here, because they know the words, '*It looks like I've got two dicks.*'

Gobbler's left leg gone from above the knee – which is called a transfemoral amputation – this allowing him to repeatedly assert a lie that keeps him happy, or relatively so.

There are six of them today: Gobbler, Petey, Fezman, Jason, Frank and Dan. That's two transfemoral – one with a transtibial to match – an elbow disarticulation, a transradial, a double wrist disarticulation – Frank's been hopeless at knitting ever since – and then there's Dan: he's a right foot disarticulation and a right arm transhumeral – roughly halfway between the elbow and the shoulder – the elbow which is not there any more and the shoulder which is – the elbow which Dan still feels – the elbow which is very often wet: warm and wet, like it was when he last saw it. This is another variety of repeatedly-asserted lie.

'Here we go, then. Where'd you get the trunks from, Fezman?' This from Jason who's hidden by the lockers nearest the exit.

'Girlfriend.'

'Got the DILAC trunks from his girlfriend, everyone.' When they move out for the main event, Jason will be on one side of Petey and Fezman will be on the other. They will cradle him, but won't talk about it. They will look mainly straight ahead. They will halt when they get to the footbath and threaten to dip in Petey's arse. This will make them laugh.

'He doesn't have a bloody girlfriend.' Gobbler again – a man who's fond of the chat, who probably was the same before.

Jason answers him from the footbath, 'Ah, but he's definitely got the trunks. Got it the wrong way round again, Fez, you minging big window-licker. You want to have the girlfriend and fuck the trunks.'

'No. I want to fuck the *girlfriend* and *have* the trunks.'

They're all giggling, Dan can hear from every side, pissing themselves over nothing, letting themselves get daft, because that's what they want.

Gobbler's all set now for his own trip to the poolside. So, 'Come and get it then, you big Marys.'

Gobbler calls for him exactly as Dan drops his locker key, has to reach it back up, pin it to his trunks without stabbing anything precious. He removes his foot before swimming. In the thickness of the water he can feel he doesn't know it isn't there, but meanwhile he grabs on to the lockers to make his way, works himself round the houses in hops and sways like he does at home.

The other two are waiting by the time he reaches them.

Then Dan and Frank and Gobbler huddle up and start to stumble themselves along – four feet between them out of the possible six.

'Mind where you put your hand, ducky. None of that 3 Para Mortar Platoon stuff here.' Gobbler sways them too close to a wall and then back.

Dan isn't much of a talker except out on the Gatherings, 'Make your bloody mind up, Gobbler.' The rest of the time he'll maybe ask for his stop on a bus, or say something mumbly and stupid to Doris at the chipper, because she wants him to be guilty and he agrees. Probably in her mind she has the truth that there's a set amount of death and what missed Dan has found another. She misunderstands the working of that truth, but he won't help her to figure it out. It's none of her business. 'Are you scared that *we're* gay, or are you just worried about yourself?' And Dan maybe does eat more chips than he should.

'Because we've always thought *you* were a fudge packer.' He could give them a miss and not have to meet her again. 'Didn't want to say so in case you got upset.' Except she needs him to be there, he can feel that. 'You'll just end up crying and then your mascara'll run.' He needs it, too.

Frank listens and smiles down at a skinny coffin-dodger who's folding his kecks on the bench nearest to them and trying to act invisible. Frank enunciates very clearly past Gobbler's ear, 'I can give you a special hand job, help you decide – clear all your pipework.' He waggles his free stump and winks. 'Just bend over and kiss Danny's ring.'

They stagger on, holding tight, and under other circumstances it might simply be that they're drunk already and out somewhere late at night – it might be there's years not happened yet and they've some other reason for being mates.

Hospital – great place to meet folk, get new mates.

Get proper pals.

Once they're out by the pool, Dan breathes in warm and wet and is harmed by the sharp light and the din from kids, hard noises.

It seems a school party is here, maybe a couple – lots of primary age heads and bodies – the water's splitting and heaving with them – all polystyrene floats and nervous piss.

Dan is aware they could prove to have an overwhelming nature, could defeat him, and he never does handle this bit too well. The shock is up and in him before he can jump and be ears full of water, wrapped by it and washed and free. He concentrates on being glad of Frank and Gobbler: the carrying, discomfort, distraction.

And he knows that once he's swimming he'll be fine. These days he goes on his back and is quite accomplished, purposeful, almost steers in the directions he intends.

'Nearly there, then.'

'Well, I had actually guessed that, you mong – cos of the fucking pool being right fucking here.' Gobbler shifts his weight and they stagger to the edge faster than intended.

Dan makes a point of exhaling and starting to grin. He is about to improve himself. He has grasped the theory, read the leaflets – people like him need a way to ignore their reminders, the signs of trauma which are their obvious and inconvenient new shape. His body is not an aid to mental rehabilitation. So he swims, makes everything glide and be easy. This means he'll improve more quickly. But not as quickly as he would without his injuries. That's a medical fact – if he still had his foot and the rest of his arm, he'd be finding life much better than he is.

He frowns, brings his thinking forward, peers ahead of his skin and his skull to the spot where Pete is already bobbing, hand at rest on the side and looking up at a woman who is pacing and speaking to Fezman and Jason. They are both still dry and standing on the tiles, Fezman in these mad, knee-length trunks like he's going to play football in the 1920s but with day-glo palm trees and dolphins and surf on them. You can tell he fancies himself in them and they're new. They maybe are from a girlfriend.

The speaking woman is round-shouldered and wears a blouse and a long skirt so tight it almost stops her walking, only this isn't good because she has no arse, no pleasantness to see – except that, when she turns away and faces Dan, he ends up looking right at the curve of her little belly and her little mound and he doesn't want to think of them. They make him sad. Everything about her is sad – browny grey and bloody depressing – hair, clothes, shoes that she clips and quarter-steps along in – and Dan can tell she's a teacher, because she's got that fakecheerful thing about her mouth and darty little eyes that are tired and want to find mistakes. Every now and then, her lips thin together and it gets obvious that her job has gone badly for her, and probably also her life. And here she is taking her class for swimming lessons on a Tuesday afternoon – for safety and fitness and possibly something else that she can't quite control. Dan is of the opinion that she should not have any kind of care over children.

'Excuse me.' The teacher doesn't speak to Dan, although she has left the others and drawn really near to him. She's maybe only in her forties, but he notices she smells of old lady.

'Excuse me.' She focuses on Gobbler. 'I realise you've been here, that you come here quite often . . .' She swallows and angles her head away, starts seriously watching the children – you'd think they were going to catch on fire, or something – not that she'd be any use to save them. 'And I've explained you to them, but now –'

'What d'you say, love?' Gobbler interrupts her and his arm around Dan flexes. 'You've explained . . . ?'

'Yes, I could explain *you* to them.'

Gobbler's arm getting ready for something, thoughts roaring about inside it, Dan can almost hear them.

'Don't know what you mean though, love. How you'd explain me. What you'd be explaining.' Gobbler is nearly giggling which the woman shouldn't think is him being friendly, because Dan knows he's not. 'Is that like I need translating? Like I'm a foreign language, because that's not it – British me, British to the core.'

Dan wanting to clear off out of it, avoid, and also wanting to do what he must, what he does – he goes along with the lads: Fezman, Frank, Jason, even Petey in the water, they close up alongside Gobbler, make a sort of line, and they watch the woman regret herself, but still think she's in the right. 'It's the children – I know you can't help it – but they get upset.'

Dan's voice out of him before he realises, 'They don't look upset.'

'One of the girls was crying.'

'They look fine. Splashing away and happy. I mean, they do. I wouldn't say it, if they weren't.'

She tries hooking into Gobbler again which is unwise and Dan wonders how she managed to qualify, even get to be a teacher, when she is this thick and this shit at understanding a situation. 'I told them you were as God made you.'

'What?'

'But with so many . . . it isn't your fault, but you must see that you're disturbing.' Her hands waver in front of her, as if she can't quite bear to point at them. 'You are disturbing. I'm sorry, but you are.' She nods. 'There must be places you can go to where you'd be more comfortable.' Her fingers take hold of her wrists and cling.

And the lads don't speak.

She stays standing there and hasn't got a fucking clue.

And the lads don't speak.

Dan can tell that she has no idea they're deciding to be still, to be the nicest they can be, working up to it by deciding they will mainly forget her and what she's said and who they are.

And the lads don't speak.

She gives them a disapproving face, touch of impatience.

And Fezman nods, thoughtful, and says – he's very even, gentle with every word – says to her, 'These are new trunks. I like these trunks. They are DILAC trunks, which you don't understand.' He presses his face in mildly, mildly towards her, 'They are *Do I Look A Cunt in these trunks* trunks, and I am going to swim in them this morning. And you look a cunt and you are a cunt, you are an utter cunt and I am sorry for this, but you should know and you should maybe go away and try being different and not a cunt, but right here, right now – a cunt – you're a cunt. You are a cunt.' He nods again, slowly, and turns his face to the water and the girls and boys.

Dan watches while the woman pales and her head jumps, acts like they've spat at her, or grabbed her tits and his gone arm trembles the same way that Gobbler's does and he wants to run, can't run, wants to – wants to throw up.

The woman kind of shakes for a moment and then takes a little, hobbled step and then another, everything unsteady, leaves them.

The lads wait.

Dan sees when she reaches the opposite wall and starts yakking to a guy in a DILAC suit, guy who's standing with a *Readers' Wives* type of bint – they're colleagues, no doubt, fellow educators. He decides that he has no interest in what may transpire.

Dan and the lads take a breath, the requisite steps, and drop themselves into the water. They join Pete. They swim – show themselves thrashing, ugly, wild.

Dan watches the ceiling tiles pass above him and has his anger beneath him, has it pushing at the small of his back, bearing him up. It wouldn't be safe anywhere else.

And he makes sure that he checks – regularly checks – twists and raises his head and strains to see, makes sure that the kids have cleared out of his way, out of everyone's. He wants no accidents.

In his heart, though, in his one remaining heart, there is a depth, a wish that some morning there *will* be an accident: a frightened kid, scared boy, choking and losing his way. When this happens Dan will be there and will rescue him.

He practises in his head and in the water – the paths that his good arm will take, the grip, the strength he's already developed in his legs.

When this happens it will mean he recovers himself again – becomes a man who would save a boy, who would always intend and wish to do that – would not be any other man than the man who would do that, who would be vigilant, be a brave bastard and take care. He would never have done the thing that he couldn't have done. He never would.

No tricks of the darkness, no sounds in the pre-light,

no panic, no confusion, no walking downstairs to find it, to see how it lies like it's frightened and shouldn't be hurt. No mistake.

There should be no mistake.

There should be no mistake.

There should be no mistake.

CONTRIBUTORS

LIN ANDERSON

Lin Anderson was born in Greenock, where her father was a Detective Inspector in Greenock CID. She is an award-winning screenwriter, and author of five acclaimed crime novels featuring forensic scientist Dr Rhona MacLeod: *Torch*, *Deadly Code*, *Driftnet*, *Dark Flight* and the latest, *Easy Kill*. She lives in Edinburgh.

www.lin-anderson.com

KATE ATKINSON

Kate Atkinson was born in York and now lives in Edinburgh. Her first novel, *Behind the Scenes at the Museum*, won the Whitbread Book of the Year Award. She is the author of a collection of short stories, *Not the End of the World*, and of the critically acclaimed novels *Human Croquet*, *Emotionally Weird*, *Case Histories*, and *One Good Turn*. *Case Histories* introduced her readers to Jackson Brodie, former police inspector turned private investigator. The bestselling *One Good Turn* and new novel *When Will There Be Good News* also feature Jackson Brodie.

www.kateatkinson.co.uk

MARGARET ATWOOD

Margaret Atwood is Canada's pre-eminent novelist and poet, and author of many short stories, critical studies, screenplays, radio scripts and books for children. Her novels *Alias Grace*, *The Handmaid's Tale* and *Cat's Eye* were all shortlisted for the Booker Prize, which she won in 2000 with *The Blind Assassin*. Her work has been translated into over 30 languages, and her latest book is *Payback: Debt and the Shadow Side of Wealth*. She lives in Toronto.

www.owtoad.com

CHRISTOPHER BROOKMYRE

Christopher Brookmyre was raised in Barrhead, attended Glasgow University, and supports St Mirren F.C. He is the creator of investigative journalist Jack Parlabane, and author of twelve bestselling novels, including *Quite Ugly One Morning*, *One Fine Day in the Middle of the Night*, *All Fun and Games Until Somebody Loses an Eye*, and his new novel *A Snowball in Hell*. He has won a Critics' First Blood Award, two Sherlock Awards for Best Comic Detective and the Bollinger Everyman Wodehouse Prize for Comic Fiction.

www.brookmyre.co.uk

JOHN BURNSIDE

John Burnside has published six works of fiction and eleven collections of poetry, including *The Asylum Dance,* which won the 2000 Whitbread Poetry Award. His memoir, *A*

Lie About My Father, was published in 2006 to enormous critical acclaim, and was chosen as the Scottish Arts Council Non-fiction Book of the Year and the Saltire Society Scottish Book of the Year. His latest novel is *Glister*, and a second memoir is forthcoming. He is a reader in Creative Writing at St Andrew's University, and lives in Fife.

ISLA DEWAR

Isla Dewar is the hugely popular author of fourteen novels, including *It Could Happen To You*, *Giving Up On Ordinary*, *Two Kinds of Wonderful* and *Women Talking Dirty*, which was made into a film starring Helena Bonham Carter. Born in Edinburgh, she lives in Fife with her husband, a cartoonist.

A.L. KENNEDY

A.L. Kennedy's *Day* won the 2007 Saltire Scottish Book of the Year Award, the 2008 Costa Book of the Year Award and the 2008 Austrian State Prize for European Literature. She is the author of five novels, four short story collections and two works of non-fiction, and performs regularly as a stand-up comic. Her previous acclaimed novels include *Paradise*, *So I Am Glad* and *Everything You Need*. She lives in Glasgow.

www.a-l-kennedy.co.uk

DENISE MINA

Denise Mina's debut, *Garnethill*, won a John Creasey Dagger for Best First Crime Novel, and was followed by *Exile* and *Resolution*. She is best known for her ongoing series of crime novels featuring female Glaswegian journalist Paddy Meehan, which began in 2005 with *The Field of Blood*. She has also written a graphic novel, and a number of plays and radio dramas. The latest Paddy Meehan novel is *The Last Breath*. She has taught criminology and criminal law, and researched a PhD thesis on the ascription of mental illness to female offenders. She lives in Glasgow.

www.denisemina.co.uk

IAN RANKIN

Ian Rankin was born in Fife and studied at the University of Edinburgh. He is the U.K.'s leading crime author, whose bestselling Inspector Rebus novels have been translated into over twenty languages, won many prizes in the U.K., the U.S.A. and Europe, and have been adapted into a major television series.

He has written nineteen books in the Rebus series – the latest is *Exit Music* – as well as seven stand-alone novels and a collection of short stories. His most recent novel is *Doors Open*.

Ian Rankin was recently awarded the O.B.E. for services to literature, opting to receive the award in his home city of Edinburgh, where he lives with his partner and two sons.

www.ianrankin.net

JAMES ROBERTSON

James Robertson is the author of three acclaimed novels: *The Fanatic*, *Joseph Knight* – which won both major Scottish literary prizes: the Saltire Scottish Book of the Year and the Scottish Arts Council Book of the Year – and *The Testament of Gideon Mack*, which was featured on 'Richard & Judy's Book Club', and longlisted for the 2006 Man Booker Prize.

He has also published short stories, poetry, anthologies, essays and translations into Scots, and has compiled a *Dictionary of Scottish Quotations*.

He is a recipient of the prestigious Creative Scotland Award, and in 2004 served as the Scottish Parliament's first Writer in Residence. He lives in Angus.

IRVINE WELSH

Irvine Welsh shot to fame with *Trainspotting*, which became a worldwide bestseller, and was followed by six novels and three collections of short stories.

He is the author of a number of plays and screenplays, and his latest novel is *Crime*.

Irvine Welsh was born in Edinburgh, and now divides his time between his home city, Miami Beach and Dublin.

www.irvinewelsh.net